Order of Merit

Richard Storry

ISBN: 1517296838

ISBN 13: 9781517296834

By the same author:
The Cryptic Lines

First published: 2015 by Cryptic Publications.

Cover design by Gergö Pocsai

Order of Merit

Prologue

The weeping of the guitar begins.
Useless to silence it.
It weeps monotonously
as water weeps,
as the wind weeps over snowfields.
Impossible to silence it.
It weeps for distant things.
Arrow without target.
Oh, guitar!
Heart mortally wounded.

\- Federico Garcia Lorca

Chapter One

London - 1978

It was the first day of his adult life and Marcus Hyde, now exactly eighteen years and no days old, was feeling deliriously happy.

For years he had been looking forward to the day when he could finally have an alcoholic drink, legally, and go to see any movie that appealed without having to lie to the ticket seller about his age. He was basically a good kid - he just got into the occasional spot of bother; nothing serious - just the sorts of things that any growing lad would do; and he'd lost count of the number of times his parents (especially his dad) had told him to get on with his guitar and piano practice. In fact, as the years had progressed, he had developed into a very able musician and was thrilled to find that he had been offered a place at the Royal Academy of Music, starting in September. His parents were simultaneously delighted and relieved. His course in life was set. All was well.

And now, his big day had finally arrived and he was eighteen years old at last. He walked across Crystal Palace park, along the Parade and then turned right, taking brisk strides towards the brasserie in Westow Hill where he had arranged to meet his father. In the back of his mind he wished that both his parents might have been willing to set aside their differences for at least one afternoon and celebrate his birthday together, but he was by now quite accustomed to seeing them separately, and he was determined to enjoy himself, today of all days.

This area of suburban London was built on high ground. Indeed, the gentle breezes which would frequently sweep in from the adjoining county of Kent (also known as *The Garden of England*) had helped the area to acquire the title of 'the fresh air suburb'. It was a very pleasant place to live. From his high vantage point, Marcus could look down on the rest of London, stretching away into the distance. It was an endless carpet of buildings, some old (in a wide variety of architectural styles) some new (provoking differing opinions as to how aesthetically pleasing they were) and some partially built, along with the numerous parks and, on the horizon, the famous transmitter mast at Alexandra Palace.

Sporting his new pair of blue Levis and a cream coloured sweatshirt, both of which were birthday gifts from relatives, he had a broad smile on his face as he confidently swung open the door to Bruciani's and stepped inside, immediately aware of the chattering customers and smelling the distinctive aroma of freshly ground coffee.

"Hey Marcus!" The voice called above all the clatter. "I hear congratulations are in order?"

Bruce, resplendent in his trademark red and white striped apron, stood behind the counter, a rather rotund but extremely good natured fellow. Marcus had always liked him. He raised his voice to make himself heard above both the ambient background noise and the occasional crash which emanated from the kitchen through the archway.

"Yeah, you better watch out 'cos today I have officially become...a man!"

"Ooh, yes sir, anything you say, sir."

They smiled and shook hands.

"Since it's your special day," began Bruce, "go ahead and order anything you like - it's my treat." He handed him the attractively printed menu, but then his expression changed and he wagged a warning finger. "Only today, mind you. I don't want you thinking you can just waltz in here for a freebie any day of the week."

"Thanks Bruce, you're a pal."

Marcus took the menu and made his way across the light brown, slightly uneven parquet floor. Some of the tiles were a little loose and moved slightly when they were walked on, but that just added to the character of this quaint establishment. Moving past the other diners, Marcus reached the corner table, in its own small alcove and set perfectly for two, and noticed, with satisfaction, that Bruce had already placed one of his 'reserved' signs there.

What Marcus liked about this charming, characterful place was that, every time you visited, old Bruce somehow managed to create the illusion that he and his establishment existed exclusively for your benefit. He was always so friendly, and the tables were always laid so neatly. But there was a second reason too: Bruciani's chocolate fudge cake was unsurpassed - according to the menu, it was 'world famous'; and, although Marcus hadn't ever actually encountered this delicacy-a-la-Brucie anywhere else, he wasn't going to argue about it.

He glanced at his watch – also a birthday gift, and a fine timepiece indeed: an Omega Aquaterra. His dad would be here in a few minutes and they could begin what had become, for them, a birthday ritual. They would start with a combo platter for two - a veritable cornucopia of chicken wings, garlic mushrooms, calamari and prawns, each with its own dedicated creamy dipping sauce which brought a mouth-watering succulence to each element - before proceeding to a sixteen-ounce sirloin steak and fries with all the trimmings. The steak would be topped with a triumphant peppercorn sauce; and the fries were not just any fries – these were double cooked according to the renowned Bruciani method: firstly lowered reverently into the purest cooking oil and then subsequently fried to perfection. Marcus took his steak medium but his dad's would be well done. Most importantly, owing to the uniqueness of this particular birthday, in the only departure from what had become the norm, they would both be having a large glass of beer, or possibly two, to accompany the meal. And finally, just when they thought they couldn't squeeze in another morsel, it would be time for a giant slice of the 'world famous' chocolate fudge cake, bedecked with ice cream and chocolate sauce, all homemade according to Bruce's secret family recipe. In the past Marcus had asked Bruce why he didn't simply buy in his ice cream ready-made, but Bruce was adamant that it was simply 'not the done thing' to serve up anything to his customers other than what had been carefully made on the premises. So far, no one had disagreed with him and that trend seemed sure to continue for quite some time yet. To complete the gastronomic experience, Marcus was determined to try a liquor coffee. He'd never even considered it before; actually, he had always thought of it as being an 'old man's drink'. However, now that he was a man (albeit not an old one yet) he could do whatever he wanted. He scanned the menu, just in case anything else should grab his attention, but he knew that the main component parts of the meal were already decided.

Glancing up, he noticed a burly, unpleasant looking man speaking in low tones to Bruce across the counter. He was wearing a suit which was clearly expensive but which did not fit well, and made him look awkward. Marcus hadn't seen him arrive and it was difficult to hear what was being said over the general hubbub of the cafe, but it was clear that this was not a friendly conversation. Bruce was looking decidedly ill-at-ease and Marcus began hoping even more fervently that his dad would arrive very soon.

At the counter, Bruce was speaking in a low voice, trying to avoid attracting glances from the customers.

"It's OK, Luther, tell him not to worry," he stammered. "I'll have it ready by tomorrow, honest. I just don't have it here right now, that's all."

Slowly and deliberately, Luther reached over and grabbed the front of Bruce's apron in his two huge fists, half lifting him across the counter. He regarded him for a long moment, and when he spoke again Bruce found himself inhaling a lungful of his stale breath.

"Zoltan doesn't give credit, Brucie boy, you know that."

"I know...I know," he gasped. "It's just -"

"What's going on here?"

The sudden loud question caused all conversations in the cafe to cease and was accompanied by a hand placed firmly on the shoulder of Luther who released his grip on Bruce and spun round to find himself looking into the firm gaze of this new arrival: tall, in his early forties and on the slim side of medium. He assessed the man briefly and snorted.

"I don't know who you are, slimeball, but you better mind your own business if you wanna keep that pretty face of yours in one piece." With a sneer, he shook himself free from the hand on his shoulder and turned back to Bruce again but before he could speak the hand was returned to his shoulder, more firmly this time. He spun round once more, angry now.

"Don't you speak English? I thought I told you -"

But before he could utter another word the man's fist slammed deep into his solar plexus and he reeled back against the counter. There were gasps from the startled customers.

"You take your lousy protection racket and clear off right now! Are you hearing me? And you tell your boss that we aren't going to tolerate his kind in our area. Do I make myself clear?"

Over in his corner of the cafe, although he was feeling a little unsettled by the whole incident, Marcus watched as his father took control of the situation and felt a glow of pride. His dad glanced across to him and gave one of those little winks that Marcus had always liked. He smiled back, but then his eyes suddenly widened in horror.

"Dad, look out!"

But it was too late. That one moment of distraction was all it took.

The pistol, looking small in Luther's large hand, coughed just once, and Dave Hyde staggered, a look of surprise on his face, and grabbed the edge of the counter before slowly sliding to the floor. Customers screamed and dived under tables.

"NO!"

Marcus was out of his seat and racing towards Luther in a blind rage. He leapt onto the man's back and landed several punches, which appeared to have no effect whatsoever. Luther roared and spun round, dislodging his assailant and delivering a well-placed roundhouse punch which sent Marcus sprawling to the floor in a daze. As he tried to regain his senses, he looked up to find himself staring straight into the muzzle of the pistol.

"Luther, don't do it, please don't. He's only a boy!" Bruce begged from behind the counter.

Luther didn't move. His hand was steady and his face was grim.

"Luther, please!"

Luther's lip curled into another sneer, and Marcus saw the man's knuckle whiten as he began to squeeze the trigger, and he closed his eyes. Just then, from outside, the sound of police sirens could be heard drawing nearer. Luther glanced at Bruce and then back at Marcus.

"You're one lucky kid," he hissed. Then, to Bruce, he said, "We'll be back, you know, and Zoltan isn't gonna be pleased."

With that, he turned and lurched towards the door, with one hand still clutching his stomach. As he passed the end of the counter he snarled and reached out his other arm, swiping a large display of multi-coloured cupcakes onto the floor. As the door slammed behind him Bruce immediately grabbed the phone and called for an ambulance while, ignoring his own pain, Marcus crawled across the floor to his dad. There was blood everywhere. His breathing was shallow and his face was deathly pale.

"Dad..."

As customers began cautiously emerging from under their tables, Dave Hyde attempted a smile.

"Hey Marcus, welcome to the wonderful world of adulthood. Sorry about all this. It's not much of a birthday present is it?" He spoke with difficulty.

"Don't try to talk; the ambulance will be here soon."

"Son...I...I don't think it'll be here in time."

Marcus' eyes filled with tears.

"Don't say that, dad. Stay with me, OK? Just stay with me."

"I love you, Marcus."

His eyes closed and his head slowly turned to one side.

"No, dad, no!"

As police cars screeched to a halt outside the brasserie, Marcus, in front of an audience of shell-shocked customers, flung himself across his father's lifeless body and wept.

Chapter Two

1990

"...and now I'd like you to listen to this short piece of music, after which I shall ask you what you noticed about the dynamics, and whether you can suggest approximately when it might have been written."

The exam candidate nodded and the music examiner began to play. The youngster was taking her Grade 5 piano exam and, having completed all the other sections, the final part was now in progress - the aural tests. After playing the piece, with the candidate listening carefully, the examiner asked:

"At the beginning, was the music loud or quiet?"

"Quiet."

"And did it stay like that throughout?"

"No, it gradually got louder."

"And do you think it was composed during the baroque period, the romantic period or the twentieth century?"

"Romantic."

"And why do you choose that particular one?"

"'Cos romantic music is always long and boring."

The examiner, professional to the core, retained an impassive outward demeanour. He had heard so many answers of this sort, from many of the thousands of candidates he had examined over the years, that nothing could ruffle him. Inwardly, though, on this occasion he felt just a little peeved.

Long and boring? How could she say that? I played it with my heart!

Nevertheless, he threw on his best professional smile and said, "Thank you, and that's the end of the exam. Thanks for coming, and please remember to take all your music with you."

The girl turned and left the room, po-faced and without a word, causing the examiner to wonder, once again, whether politeness and common courtesy were indeed becoming lost skills.

Returning to his desk he quickly completed the report form and totalled the marks: 102 out of 150. Since the minimum pass mark was 100 she had just scraped through. Well, her granny would probably be pleased for her.

There was a gentle knock and the exam steward, a sweet little old lady of about 75, popped her head round the door.

"Are you ready for the last candidate of the day?"

"Yes. Please show him in."

He glanced down at his door list. Someone called Joshua McDaniel was about to take his Grade 8 piano exam; and then...well, then the examiner would be going back to his hotel to have a gin and tonic, before taking a dip in the pool and then relaxing the evening away with a delicious gourmet meal and several glasses of claret. He looked up again as the boy, who appeared to be in his mid-teens, entered the room just a little nervously; yet there was a confidence too, and he was immaculately turned out.

"Hello, Joshua. Please sit down at the piano and make yourself comfortable. Would you like to begin with your pieces or your scales?"

"Pieces, please."

"Certainly, and which is your first one going to be?"

"*Dem Andenken Petofis*, by Liszt."

"Thank you. Please start when you're ready."

As he placed his hands on the keys it was immediately apparent that this performance was going to be a good one. Joshua's entire body language conveyed focus, intent and commitment, and he commanded attention. From the soulful, single-line melody which began the piece, throughout the gradually thickening musical texture, and building right up to the magical fortissimo climax, the piece was delivered with such passion and polish that the examiner had no difficulty in awarding the performance full marks, which was a rare thing to do; and the rest of the exam continued in a similar vein: the Mozart *Allegro Moderato* was presented with a delightfully stylistic lightness of touch, and his interpretation of the Scarlatti *Sonata* displayed plenty of well controlled finger agility. Even his scales and arpeggios were silky smooth and seemed effortless. After that came the sight-reading test, which often struck fear into the hearts of many candidates. He, however, after romping through it as though it was a mere formality, then gave such accurate and informed responses to the aural tests, that they were about as far removed from the previous candidate as it was possible to get. The examiner always enjoyed hearing candidates like this - he felt like he was somehow contributing to the greater good when he was able to award a pass with distinction – the highest level available.

"Thank you, and that's the end of the exam. Thanks for coming, and please remember to take all your music with you."

Joshua hesitated.

"Just before I go, can I ask you a question?"

The examiner was immediately on guard. Whenever a candidate wanted to ask a question like this it was always the same: "Did I pass?" or "Can you tell me how well I did?" ...and, of course, to give an answer to such a question was not allowed.

"Er...yes, what's your question?" The subsequent reply took him a little by surprise.

"Can you tell me, how can I get to be an examiner like you?"

There was something about those last two words that somehow hit home. How can I get to be an examiner *like you?*

He raised an eyebrow. "You want to be an examiner?"

Joshua nodded.

"How old are you?"

"Seventeen."

"OK, well, you need to learn a second instrument."

"I already play the guitar to Grade 6."

"Really? Well, that's a good start. In addition I would advise you to participate in as many other musical activities as you can. Try to play in some ensembles as well as just by yourself. If your school has a choir, join it. Then, after you finish your schooling you should aim to go to university or music college and get a degree. By the time you've completed that you'll probably have some students of your own, as well as being involved in doing numerous concerts; and perhaps you'll be writing music of your own as well."

Joshua was obviously listening intently.

"...And, once you have a good selection of musical activities going on, that would be the time to contact the head office and ask if they'll see you for an interview."

"Thank you, sir, I appreciate it. Can I shake your hand?"

They shook hands and maintained eye contact for a long moment – something that slightly surprised them both.

As Joshua turned to leave, the examiner departed slightly from pro-cedure as he said, "Good luck, Josh. Work hard and perhaps we'll meet again in the future."

Joshua smiled. "Thank you," he said, simply, then left the room, clos-ing the door softly behind him.

Chapter Three

1996

The performance was going satisfyingly well, and there were only a few minutes to go until the interval. As the guitarist reached the end of the fourth of *Five Bagatelles* by William Walton, the thought occurred to him, once again, that it was a great shame that Walton had not gone on to write anything further for the instrument. He had a way of handling harmony that was unique to him and somehow seemed to capture a delightfully English quality, despite references to other countries along the way, and all bound together with an undeniable musical integrity - a veritable genius. Back in his student days, one of the performer's old professors used to say that the guitar was a better instrument than most of the music written for it. This was, perhaps, something of a sweeping statement but it was certainly true that really good guitar pieces were as a drop in the musical ocean when compared to the repertory of an instrument such as the piano, for instance.

The performer always enjoyed performing at the Purcell Room, part of London's South Bank Centre and, as he played the final *tambor* chord of the fourth bagatelle, he waited, silent and motionless, as the sound slowly faded away. You could have heard a pin drop. After a long moment he relaxed and began to quietly check his tuning. The audience took this as their cue to move a little in their seats and get comfortable again before the breathtaking finale began.

The fifth bagatelle, it must be said, makes intense demands on the player. It contains virtually continuous semiquavers, at a fast tempo, with plenty of shifts for the left hand. It is not a piece to be approached lightly but, in the right hands, it is a real crowd pleaser. Also, as the recitalist knew full well, there was nothing that pleased a crowd more than seeing a player working himself virtually to death; and he had no intention of disappointing his audience. In any case, he wanted to do all he could to ensure that they came back in after the interval to hear his sublime interpretation of Bach's famous D-minor Chaconne. And then...*then*, if he was really lucky, they might even buy one of his numerous recordings on sale in the foyer after the concert was finally over.

Sitting in a pool of bright light on the otherwise darkened stage, he was aware of the crowd but couldn't actually see them. This was just the way he liked it. The fidgeting subsided and an expectant silence ensued. The guitarist took a deep breath and focused. Then, suddenly, he launched himself into the fortissimo opening with such bravura and showmanship that the helpless audience were immediately won over without a fight. They watched, spellbound, as the semiquavers were fired with meticulous precision. The player was pleased. Things didn't always run quite as planned but on this occasion he was having a good night. His pacing was flawless, and he gauged his crescendos so perfectly that he even impressed himself. As he delivered the final tempestuous descending passage, the rapturous applause began even before the last chord had stopped. He looked up with one of his trademark beaming smiles and stood to receive his well-deserved acclaim, before giving a deep appreciative bow. With another smile, he turned and left the spotlight, heading back into the wings. After a moment the applause faded as the loudspeaker announced,

"Ladies and gentlemen, there will now be a fifteen-minute interval. Fifteen minutes, please. Thank you."

The stunned audience began to shuffle in the direction of the various bars and kiosks out in the foyer.

The date for the concert had been chosen with care. The Purcell Room shared its stage door with the Queen Elizabeth Hall, but there was no concert in the QEH tonight. The skeleton staff assigned to cover the Purcell Room gig had disappeared once the lighting check was finished, and wouldn't be needed again until after the performance was over, so there was no one around – just as he had intended.

14 minutes...

As the guitarist returned to his dressing room he carefully placed his E.B.Jones concert guitar back in its Davies case, before reaching under the chaise longue and removing another rather smaller case which he had secretly placed there earlier. After checking that his dressing room door was locked he unfastened the two metal clasps and eased open the lid.

13 minutes...

He gave a slight smile as he reached into the case and withdrew the model 625 Smith and Wesson. He hefted it for a moment before also taking the silencer that had been lying alongside it and fitting it to the muzzle with practised ease. He put on his long overcoat, which was well able to conceal the weapon in one of its numerous voluminous pockets, then quietly unlocked the door. He knew there would be no one nearby but he exercised caution all the same.

12 minutes...

As he expected, the lobby area was clear, so he made a beeline for the doorway leading to the square-spiral stairs down to the stage door. Taking a ninety degree turn to the right after every eight steps he quickly passed the floor where the QEH bar, which would normally be bustling with people, stood quiet and dark. He continued down and, a few moments later reached the glass partition behind which the stage door-keeper kept watch. But not tonight; there appeared to be no one on duty.

11 minutes...

The guitarist tapped in the code on the keypad by the door-keeper's office and entered, quickly moving over to the ante-room where the door-keeper hung his coat and made his tea. During a very friendly chat earlier today, he had been most appreciative when the guitarist had offered to make him his tea, - and now there he was, out cold, lying on the couch just as he had been left, sleeping like a baby. The guitarist nudged him but there was no response. He gave a little nod of satisfaction. The poor cove would be out for hours.

Upstairs in the foyer, the crowd was positively buzzing with excitement about the quality of tonight's concert. Conversations were interrupted momentarily as the loudspeaker announced, "Ladies and gentlemen, tonight's performance will resume in ten minutes. Ten minutes, please. Thank you."

The performer quickly exited the office, turned left and headed out of the building into the catacomb that was the network of walkways and car-parks beneath the South Bank Centre, a hub of cultural delights. As well as being home to the National Film Theatre, the Purcell Room and Queen Elizabeth Hall, there were also three other theatres on site, as well as the world renowned Royal Festival Hall. It was towards the car-park of the latter that the guitarist now headed. As he drew near, he paused and glanced round to make certain he was alone. In the distance a group of skate-boarders practised their tricks in one of the covered areas, occasionally applauding each other's efforts in that 'male bonding' sort of way. A little nearer, a homeless man sat slumped against a wall, head down, holding a brown paper bag with a bottle protruding from it.

Satisfied that there was no one close enough to see and identify him, the guitarist continued into the dimly lit covered car-park, looking for his quarry. It wasn't hard to find: the Bentley stood out like a sore thumb in the midst of all those cheaper vehicles and, just as he had been informed, the chauffeur was there behind the wheel, waiting patiently for his boss who was at this moment enjoying beluga caviar with champagne on ice in his private box in the recently refurbished concert hall, as the Royal Philharmonic Orchestra gave a spectacular performance of Tchaikovsky's fourth symphony.

9 minutes...

The chauffeur had wound down the window of the Bentley and sat with his elbow resting on the frame as he took a drag from the final cigarette in the packet. When his boss had left him the packet had been full. He cursed and dropped the empty packet onto the tarmac. It had to be said, he didn't quite *look* like a chauffeur. He was wearing the uniform, yes, but it didn't really fit properly and his straggly hair stuck out from under his smart peaked cap; and his musical tastes were definitely not the same as those of his boss. True, he was not yet elderly, but neither was he especially young, so the hideous screeching of *Twisted Sister* blaring and thumping from the car's hi-tech speaker system was, in such a fine automobile, incongruous...and very loud. The guitarist, now standing less than ten feet away and concealed behind a concrete pillar, didn't mind.

8 minutes...

One of the chauffeur's duties was to keep the car pristine and immaculate at all times, so that his boss always had a gleaming, impressive vehicle in which to travel around and attend to his business. And that was one respect in which the chauffeur did do his job well. He sat, listening to his favourite 'music', mouthing along to what passed for lyrics and drumming his fingers on the top edge of the lowered window. He allowed himself a moment of self-appreciation and mumbled, "You certainly landed on your feet with this job, Luther. Good boy. Good boy." With smug satisfaction he looked around at the spotlessly clean upholstery, the polished paintwork and the sparkling windscreen.

A fraction of a second later, the remains of that same windscreen were splattered with blood and bone as the bullet, which had entered the chauffeur's skull just behind the right ear, exited through his left eye socket and continued on its way, blasting through the glass and embedding itself in the nearby concrete wall. The chauffeur sat upright and motionless, his one remaining eye staring sightlessly ahead, with the morbid lyrics of *Twisted Sister* mocking him. The guitarist didn't need to inspect the body. He knew even before he had pulled the trigger that his aim was true. His job was done. Only moments later he was already re-entering the stage door of the Purcell Room.

7 minutes...

As soon as he was inside, he removed his coat, keeping the weapon carefully concealed. He had barely done so when a voice suddenly spoke, right alongside him.

"Good evening, sir! Leaving so soon?"

The suddenness and nearness of the jovial voice startled him. He spun round to see one of the lighting technicians who had helped him ready the platform earlier in the day.

"Oh, it's you! You made me jump."

"Of course I did, sir. It's my speciality."

The guitarist managed half a smile.

"I was actually wanting to have a quick word with the stage door-keeper but he doesn't seem to be here. I don't suppose you know where he might be?"

"Down the pub, most likely!" He laughed, a large, round, friendly laugh, then continued, "No, I'm afraid I dunno where he's got to. He'll be somewhere nearby – he's not allowed to leave until everyone else has left the building, so I don't think he'll be long. You could always leave him a note."

"Yes, I'll probably do that."

"Anyway, I'm on early shift today so I'm off to have a nice quiet dinner with the missus. Joe will be along soon to turn everything off after you're done. Have a good one!"

The guitarist nodded his farewell and the technician turned and pushed open the door, heading out into the night.

6 minutes...

This unexpected encounter with the technician had delayed him. Cursing under his breath, the guitarist sprinted up the numerous flights of stairs and returned to his dressing room just a little short of breath, locking the door behind him.

"Ladies and gentlemen, please return to your seats. Tonight's performance will continue in five minutes. Five minutes, please. Thank you."

Separating the silencer from the pistol, he returned both items to the case, closing and locking the lid, then carefully sliding it back out of sight beneath the ornate chaise lounges. He paused for a few moments, taking deep breaths and regaining his focus.

4 minutes...

Now turning his attention to his guitar case, he opened it and once again removed the expensive concert instrument. He sat down on the red padded stool and began to check the tuning.

3 minutes...

Satisfied, once again, that his guitar was singing beautifully, he returned it to its case and headed through the other door into the en-suite bathroom. There would be nothing worse than being caught short part-way through the Bach Chaconne - the longest single movement in the entire guitar repertoire.

2 minutes...

There was a polite tap on the door.

"Second half call, sir. Please stand by."

Picking up his beloved instrument, he opened the door and walked the few steps to the large door leading to the stage, where the stagehand was now back at his post, grinning.

"They're a good crowd tonight, sir, very appreciative. Apparently they've been saying some very nice things about you out in the foyer."

"Have they, indeed? That's most kind of them."

He smiled, quietly making one final tuning check.

1 minute...

After a few moments, the stagehand received a message in his headset. He acknowledged it and turned to the performer.

"We now have clearance, sir, so whenever you're ready."

The guitarist quickly ran a comb through his hair and made sure that his bow tie was straight. After a quick final check of his appearance in the full length mirror, he took another deep breath then gave a nod to the stagehand, who smiled again and moved the slider on his lighting desk to gently dim the auditorium lights.

There was a moment of hush from the expectant crowd, which immediately became a swell of applause as they saw the performer returning to the platform, and walking into the spotlight with a winning smile. He gave a deep yet humble bow, took his seat, waited for the audience to settle and then began what turned out to be a truly captivating performance of the Bach Chaconne.

♦ ♦ ♦

If anything, the second half of the recital was even more successful than the first. The broad, majestic quality of the Chaconne was complemented delightfully by the charming, though difficult, Sonatina by Federico Moreno-Torroba and, as a finale, the wonderfully fizzy and frothy *Gran Jota de Concierto* by Francisco Tarrega. No matter where that particular piece was performed the audience would always gasp during the snare drum section - most people had no idea that the guitar was capable of producing such a realistic effect. The short but sparkling *Rosita*, also by Tarrega, was offered as an encore. The adoring crowd would have kept him there all night, but he knew just how long to stand acknowledging the applause before turning and vacating the stage at just the right speed, with just the right size of smile and just the right degree of humility. He knew how to do his job. He was a pro, and his audience loved him for it.

Once back in the dressing room, he deftly placed all his concert gear back into the various compartments of his well-travelled gig bag, put everything else into a shoulder bag, then picked up his guitar case and was heading towards the exit within minutes. Having given a curt nod to the stage manager he descended the stairs before pausing momentarily at the door-keeper's booth to sign out. Casually glancing into the room beyond he spotted the door-keeper sitting upright and conscious but looking a little groggy, with one of the ushers offering him an aspirin and a glass of water.

The guitarist left the building with a spring in his step but, as he headed towards his car, he was stopped by a uniformed police constable.

"Sorry, sir, you can't go that way."

"Oh? Why ever not?"

"Nothing to worry about, sir, it's just that there's been a small incident."

"Really? Where? What sort of incident?"

"Just across the way, in the customers' car park."

A number of emergency vehicles could be seen, with blue lights flashing, and various people in green overalls milling about.

"Oh, but my car is in the artists' car park, just over there. I was doing the Purcell Room concert this evening."

"Oh, I'm sorry sir, I hadn't realised. Which is your vehicle, sir?"

He pointed towards the gleaming red Aston Martin.

"Well sir, you do travel in style, don't you?"

"Not really, I had to sell everything else I owned to pay for it."

The young policeman laughed.

As he turned to leave, the player paused and said, "Constable, can you tell me what happened over there?"

"I'm not really supposed to say, sir, but...well...it was a shooting, barely an hour ago."

"A shooting? Here?"

"Yes, sir. Quite a bad one. It's probably best if you get on your way before all the forensics people get here; it's going to get quite busy very soon. Funny old world, sir. A funny old world."

"Well, thanks for the advice. I think perhaps I will take my leave."

"Right you are, sir. Goodnight."

"Goodnight."

The guitar rode on the back seat; it was far too valuable to risk being knocked around with the rest of the luggage in the boot. As he loaded everything into the car he was aware of the policeman still watching him from a distance. Having stowed everything safely, he opened the driver's door and gave a cheery wave to the officer before settling himself behind the wheel. A moment later, the engine roared into life and he guided the mighty machine out of the car park, away from the South Bank complex and, moments later, was cruising just within the speed limit over Waterloo Bridge. Halfway across, he smiled to himself as he passed a convoy of police vehicles, with blue lights flashing, speeding in the opposite direction.

"A funny old world, indeed," he said, softly, and switched on BBC Radio 3 just in time to catch the final two movements from the Requiem by Gabriel Fauré.

Chapter Four

1978

Following the tragedy at Bruciani's, it wasn't a particularly long time before Marcus Hyde began to harness his grief and decide what he was really going to do. From a very early age he had displayed a high level of musical aptitude. He loved many different types and styles of music and, when he wasn't actually playing his instruments, he would be found going to concerts, frequently poring over the scores in the music library afterwards to try and ascertain how a particular musical effect had been achieved. He would obtain different recordings of the same piece of music to discover how various performers and conductors brought their own personal interpretation to a certain movement or passage; and he became fluent in composition, excelling in counterpoint and often becoming a nuisance to his contemporaries, as he would think nothing of calling someone at 11pm, or later, just to ask whether a certain combination of notes was playable on their particular instrument at such and such a tempo. He was more of a genius than he realised; and he aspired to a full time musical career, because he simply could not imagine not doing so.

But there was another contributing factor. Somehow, in the midst of all of his natural musical ability and enthusiasm, the image of his father was never far away. Marcus recalled many happy childhood moments where his father, who was no mean player himself, would exhort and encourage him constantly: "Play with your heart, Marcus. Do anything else you like - anything at all - but always play with your heart." And he did. The music may have been composed at any time from the renaissance period to the present day - it made no difference to him: His playing was instinctively authentic sounding and he played with such commitment and intensity that he naturally commanded the attention of anyone within earshot whenever he began to play. Channelling the grief from his loss, he resolved that he would honour the memory of his father by devoting all his energies to becoming the very best musician he could be. It quickly became clear to everyone that he was destined to become a player of professional standing; but, even more so, his devotion to his father caused the desire to grow within him to become the absolute leader in his field. And, as the days following his father's murder ticked by, gradually becoming months, and then years, this desire developed a second strand: the desire for revenge.

Chapter Five

1996

In his hotel room, two days after his recital at the Purcell Room, the assassin woke early. Although he did possess a very pleasant London home – one of the results of his various lucrative income streams - he preferred to make use of London's many hotels when he was on assignment. Each one was selected only after very careful assessment of its location and layout, and he never used the same hotel twice. This morning he quickly readied himself, and ate a hi-energy breakfast bar. He dressed in casual clothes, then noticed the daily newspaper which had been pushed under his door. He picked it up and was about to cast it aside when he noticed the headline, *Police admit: South Bank Shooting Carnage – still no leads.* A smile played across his lips. It was hardly carnage, he thought to himself, just a single shot right on target. Why did the media always have to exaggerate? He dropped the paper into the waste basket, then strode to the door and looked through the peep-hole to ensure the corridor was empty. He couldn't see anyone, but the range of what he could see was limited, so he was cautious as he opened the door just a crack. As with most quality hotels these days, the corridors were covered by closed circuit TV cameras, but he knew that they were hardly ever actively monitored by real human beings.

Satisfied that the coast was clear he stepped out into the corridor. He placed the 'Do not disturb' notice on the handle and closed the door, softly. Then he walked briskly to the end and turned the corner. He paused by the door to another room before producing an electronic room key to open it. As he stepped inside he again made use of the 'Do not disturb' sign. Confident that he had not been observed, he crossed to the walk-in wardrobe from which he removed a large holdall which he placed on the bed. Opening it, he removed a pair of grey overalls, lightweight boots and a cap with a wide peak.

He swiftly donned everything and stood in front of the mirror. The reflection staring back at him looked just like any maintenance man – the sort of person that would go virtually un-noticed in a place like this, and would certainly not attract undue attention from any guests. Even so, it was always wise to take as many precautions as possible. He picked up the holdall, opened the connecting door and walked into the adjoining room which had also been reserved for him. Having now altered his appearance, if anyone *had* seen him leaving his room, it was unlikely they would notice him emerging from a different one and realise that he was the same person.

From that adjacent room, he once again entered the corridor, attaching, as he did so, the same signage to the door handle as before. He padded his way silently along the carpeted corridors, arrived at the staff elevator and pushed the button. He stepped forward as the doors opened but hurriedly stepped back as a waiter with a room service trolley began to emerge. A quick glance at the trolley showed that one of the hotel guests had ordered a huge breakfast – someone with more money than sense, thought the assassin. A curt nod was exchanged as the waiter began to trundle the trolley away along the corridor. The assassin would have preferred to have made his exit without being seen by anyone, but it was unlikely that this waiter would particularly remember him. Such was the mundane nature of that type of hotel work, staff would often go through their shift as little more than automatons, smiling as instructed and delivering appropriate lines to hotel guests but actually assimilating very little of what was going on around them.

Once inside, he waited as the elevator descended all the way down to the lower basement level. The doors opened with a slight hiss and he stepped out into the staff-only area. Moving quietly but quickly, he entered the locker-room, removed a key from one of the zip pockets of the holdall and, after checking again that no one was around, he opened the numbered locker, removed the large manila envelope which had been left there for him the previous night and placed it securely inside the holdall. He smiled to himself. His contact, known only as the Professor, was thorough.

"P.Y.I.D." the Professor would always say. *Protect your identity.* "P.Y.I.D. at all costs." The assassin had done so, and had developed the perfect cover for his work. And, working together with the Professor, everything was always planned down to the last detail. Nothing was left to chance. Everything that he needed was always where it was supposed to be, at just the right time, and this time was no different. Together, they made a great team.

He left the locker-room and moved towards the exit. It was important that the time-keeper did not notice him leave. Producing his mobile phone he called the number of the staff entrance. After three rings it was answered and, as the man's attention was distracted, the assassin walked past the glass partition briskly, giving a small wave. The elderly time-keeper glanced up but continued to speak into the phone. "Hello? Hello?" The call disconnected. "Hmmph, I didn't want to talk to you anyway," he grunted to himself and went back to his tea and newspaper. By now the assassin had already stepped outside and was immediately engulfed in the crowds and absorbed by the hustle and bustle of the busy street. There were smart-suited city workers walking briskly, parents taking children to school, retailers raising the metal shutters on their shop windows, some manual workers erecting scaffolding, drivers loading and unloading, people handing out free newspapers – and an inconspicuous maintenance man.

The assassin smiled to himself. Without giving cause to anyone for so much as a second glance, he headed towards the location for the first of today's two assignments, as advised by the Professor.

In plain sight, he was completely invisible.

Chapter Six

The forgotten remains of what had at first been an exquisitely presented portion of smoked salmon and scrambled eggs sat congealing on its bone china plate in the centre of a sturdy Victorian mahogany desk. The fork was lying across the centre of the plate but the knife had somehow fallen from the edge and was now partially stuck to the desk's ornate surface.

The colossus for whom this mid-morning snack had been prepared was standing there, bristling like a bulldog and flushed with anger. Folds of flesh spilled out over his shirt collar, and buttons strained to hold together the fabric, which was already stretched too tightly across his more than ample acreage. These unenviable features, together with skin which was blotched and bloated, and with more than a hint of unpleasant body odour, belonged to an outraged Zoltan Augustus.

"Who is behind this?" he screamed. "WHO?"

It was bad enough that Luther had been wasted. That evening at the concert, until he returned to his car, he had been enjoying himself, surprisingly; but all that was ruined when he saw what had happened to his loyal chauffeur...and now two more of his men had been dispatched, both with a single bullet through the forehead. They were experienced men. How could they – how could they *both* - have been caught off-guard so easily?

"Who?" he shrieked again, the strained, high-pitched voice sounding odd, emerging as it did from such a voluminous body. He slammed an angry, thick-fingered fist onto the antique desk and began to heave his unpleasant bulk around his opulent study, all the while glaring at his bodyguard, Sven, the unfortunate fellow who had brought him the bad news, and who now stood awkwardly awaiting instructions, whilst wondering if he was about to bear the brunt of his boss' annoyance. The physical size of Sven himself could hardly have been described as diminutive, yet even he was dwarfed in the presence of the gigantic Mr Augustus, his employer.

Zoltan spoke quietly, yet darkly, an unmistakeable air of menace in his tone.

"The building was secure?" A nod from the nervous Sven.

"All the cameras and alarms were operating correctly?" Another nod. And then he bellowed. "So how did this...this infiltrator manage to gain access?"

Sven took an involuntary step backwards but rallied quickly.

"We're not certain, sir. All those normally present in the building had been thoroughly vetted and cleared. The only thing that was in any way irregular was that there had apparently been a problem with the drains and someone was called to come and attend to it."

"And this...plumber...was allowed access?"

"Yes, sir, he - "

" - against my express instructions?"

"Sir, he did have his ID, and I took the precaution of calling his company and they verified his identity."

"Well, of course they did!"

Zoltan paused in circling the study before asking, quietly, "And this drainage problem – is it now fixed?"

"Well, er, no. The blockage is still there."

"I'm surrounded by idiots!" boomed Zoltan, his face reddening with rage and a thick vein standing out on his forehead. Then he moved towards Sven until he was standing right in front of him. He raised a fat finger and poked him hard in the chest.

"Find this filthy little dungball. Find him, wherever and whoever he is, and bring him to me. Before we kill him I want to know just what his game is."

There was a pause, before Zoltan suddenly glanced up at Sven and bellowed again, "Didn't you hear me? I said find him! NOW!"

Sven nodded and walked quickly from the room, relieved to be out of the firing line, for the moment at least.

Alone in his magnificent study, Zoltan began to take slow deep breaths in an attempt to create the illusion of calm. Then, seating himself in the leather-bound swivel chair behind the mahogany desk he opened one of the numerous draws and removed a bottle of pills. He took a couple of them, washing them down with a swig of water from the crystal decanter in front of him. Then he slowly swung round and gazed through the bullet-proof window across the beautifully manicured lawns of his mansion, looking but not seeing – his mind was elsewhere. He was thinking about the killer of his men. Three of them gone. *Three* - in under 48 hours. His expression took on a grim determination. He would find this upstart. He would have him on his knees, squirming, begging for mercy, just like all the others.

"It is most unwise to cross swords with me," he hissed, "but who are you?" He paused, trying to recall the many names and faces of his numerous nefarious encounters over the years, yet his question hovered in the air, unanswered. "Who *are* you?"

Chapter Seven

Josh McDaniel was nervous, again.

He seemed to have spent his entire life up to this point in choosing to put himself into situations that made him uneasy. Walking onto a stage to give a performance made him nauseous – so why did he do it? In the days leading up to every one of his music exams he had been so on edge that he'd ended up with the runs. And on the day that he gave his first private music lesson (to a 12-year old girl) his fingers were trembling so much he could barely demonstrate a decent hand position at the keyboard.

And now?

Well, NOW he was in the waiting room at 24, Portland Place just along the road from BBC Broadcasting House in central London, at the headquarters of the world-renowned Associated Board of the Royal Schools of Music, waiting to be called into his interview to become a music examiner...and his stomach was tying itself in double knots.

So, why? He asked himself the question again. Why go through this self-inflicted torture, over and over? He smiled to himself – a sort of resigned half-smile. Of course he knew why he did it. He did it because he couldn't imagine going through life without playing music, or without a piano being within arm's reach, or without being able to give personal expression to his inner thoughts and feelings, through the incredible variety of tone and textures that music alone could provide.

Not only that but, recently, as a surprise, his father had taken him along to Steinway Hall and as soon as he walked through the door he had felt like a child at Christmas. All the pianos were standing there, proudly, with lids raised in salute, hoping to attract a new owner; but Josh knew exactly what he was looking for. He moved past all the medium-sized instruments, through the archway at the back and into the room where the full size concert instruments were kept. The atmosphere was hushed in here. Magnificent pianos lined the walls like sentinels, shiny and gleaming. Even here, though, there was a hierarchy – the further you walked, the more expensive the instruments became.

Josh had walked right to the end.

There he stood, for a long time, just gazing at the pristine example of incredible musical craftsmanship before him. He walked along its length slowly, several times, saw his reflection in the perfect finish, and the jet black and brilliant white keys...immaculate...enticing...beckoning.

Powerless to resist, he positioned himself on the beautifully crafted leather-upholstered piano stool and for a long moment just stared at the 88 keys in front of him. Then, slowly, reverently, he reached out and pressed one of the keys – just one – E above middle C, with the middle finger of his right hand, gently, very gently...and he was in musical heaven! That piano knew everything about him! It knew everything that had happened to him and it knew everything he was thinking and feeling. After a few moments, he played another note, and then another. Tentatively, he raised his left hand and added a few bass notes. *Oh, the depth! The power!* Gradually his fingers increased their speed, his hands sweeping over the keys, producing beautifully shaped cascading melodies, making full use of the dynamic range which was now available to him on this Rolls Royce of musical instruments!

He didn't know how long he had been playing but, when he eventually stopped, the sound fading away on a perfectly gauged pianissimo, he looked round to see his father standing and watching from a short distance away, along with a number of the staff in the store and several of the customers too. His father rarely smiled, but he was smiling now - at him.

"Do you like it, Josh?"

"It's the most wonderful instrument I've ever seen."

"I'm very pleased to hear you say that." There was a short pause, "because it's yours. I've just bought it for you."

He couldn't speak. He just about managed an acknowledging nod before running to his dad and throwing his arms around him.

"Now, son," said his dad, pushing him away, "we're out in public, so let's not have any of that sort of behaviour."

"Mr McDaniel?"

Joshua's reverie was broken by the voice, which belonged to a pretty secretary who had popped her head around the door.

"They're ready for you now. If you'd like to come this way?" She smiled as she held the door open for him. "You may want to bring those with you?"

She indicated his jacket, which he had slung on the back of a chair, and his briefcase standing beside it. Suddenly feeling just a little silly, as well as slightly sick, he returned to collect his personal items and then followed her out of the room, along the corridor and up a flight of stairs towards a rather grand and elaborately carved doorway. It wasn't far at all, but to Josh it felt like a 10-mile hike.

"This is the boardroom," the secretary said. "One moment, please. I'll just let them know you're here."

She slipped inside and, alone for a moment, Josh checked that his tie was straight and then, though it was not necessary, he wiped the toe of each shoe against his calves. He was just about to check his fly was closed but intercepted the downwards movement just in time as the secretary re-emerged.

"Mr McDaniel, would you like to come in?"

◆ ◆ ◆

Alone in his spacious office, Zoltan Augustus regarded the package on the table in front of him. It had been left at the gate, the maid had said. No message. No one had seen who left it. One of the groundsmen had noticed it and brought it up to the house. Its sender had been careful. Despite careful examination there were no obvious clues as to where it had come from or who had sent it. Just a small, square package, wrapped in brown paper, with his name typed – not written – onto a self-adhesive label on the top.

He had been in this game long enough to know that whatever the package contained it would not be good news, yet it was for precisely that reason he couldn't take the risk of allowing any of the staff to open it for him – after all, the contents could be just about anything, perhaps harmless, but perhaps not.

He picked it up again and hefted it, cautiously. Not much weight there, so it probably wasn't anything explosive, and no unusual odours. He placed it back on the table, took a deep breath then slowly and carefully – *so* carefully – began to peel back the sticky tape holding the wrapping paper in place. Little by little, the paper was unfastened and unfolded to reveal a small box made from thin card. As a precaution, Zoltan turned the box upside down and proceeded to gain access using a pen-knife to cut through the base – so slowly, *so* gently.

He peered through the tiny slit. No wires. No powder. It looked safe enough. Even so, it was with great caution that he prised open the base and looked inside.

The box contained a piece of folded white cloth; it could almost have been a bandage. As he carefully lifted it out he could tell there was something wrapped inside it. He laid it on the desk, gently. Paused again. Then, ever so gingerly, he began to unfold the white fabric. As he did so, and as he drew nearer to the centre of this mysterious package, blots of red began to appear on the material, faint at first but becoming deeper as he continued to unfold it. He smirked. *You trying to frighten me? I know real blood when I see it. What's this supposed to be? Your granny's lipstick?*

The red deepened further. As the last fold was lifted the contents were finally exposed and he sat back in his chair and stared at what lay before him.

Zoltan was not scared by what he saw, but he was angry.

In the middle of the large piece of white cloth sat a bullet. It was two inches long, with a pointed end, and scratched into it were the initials, '*Z.A.*'

And, scrawled on the cloth in red letters, was a message. The untidy writing read, *You're next.*

He thought for a moment before reaching for his phone and dialling a number, his blood simmering and his face filled with determination and resolve.

Chapter Eight

As the months following his father's murder slowly but surely became years, Marcus Hyde had worked like a man possessed.

His steely determination to become the very best that he could be knew no bounds, as he had devoted himself to his beloved music. The many hours of study had seemed to him like mere moments as they flew past. Whole volumes of music became embedded in his absorbent memory. All the preludes and fugues of Bach, every Beethoven sonata, and the complete collections of Chopin nocturnes and Brahms intermezzi were all assimilated swiftly, correctly, and in their entirety, with consummate ease and stylistic authenticity. The list was endless: Handel, Debussy, Grieg, Bartok, Schubert, Copland, Ravel, Gershwin, Rachmaninov – no composer was safe from his searching gaze, and all were managed with supreme artistry.

But his interest had not stopped there.

He had also attacked the repertoire of the classical guitar with just as much vigour. The concertos of Rodrigo, Villa Lobos and Poncé were as a playful excursion to him. All the great concert works from Sor, Giuliani, Torroba, Albeniz and Barrios flew from his fingers, along with his own expertly crafted transcriptions of the finest lute repertoire by John Dowland and Robert de Visée.

He had received invitations to play in London, New York, Paris, Milan, Berlin and Salzburg; and everywhere he went, his performances had been met with glowing, universal acclaim. Many students, dreaming of reaching his extraordinarily high level, constantly asked if they could come and study with him. Although he did not really have sufficient availability of time to accommodate such requests, in exceptional cases where a particular student was especially gifted, now and then he had been able to oblige with occasional one-off sessions as a sort of musical consultant.

Then, one day, he had become a music examiner.

Interestingly, it did not necessarily follow that an expert musician would also make an expert examiner; sometimes applications from very eminent proponents of the art had to be rejected for all sorts of other reasons: perhaps their manner was not sufficiently friendly; maybe they were poor at keeping to the strict time schedule; in some cases it was simply the pressure of the continuous concentration that proved too much.

None of these problems had applied to Marcus Hyde, however.

As with everything else he had put his hand to, he quickly emerged as a very efficient, amenable and fair examiner, with the head office frequently receiving letters from grateful teachers and candidates saying how much they appreciated his calming demeanour in the exam room and his thoughtful written comments afterwards.

It was, therefore, perhaps only to be expected that he would not remain as one of the rank and file for very long. Soon he had been promoted to the training panel, where he nurtured future examiners with great enthusiasm; and, not long after that, he found himself climbing the ladder and joining the moderating team where he found himself involved in ensuring parity and consistency of marking across the panel of over 600 colleagues.

When he was finally offered the post of Chief Examiner quite a lot of negotiation was involved. He was keen to take on this new and exciting challenge but did not want to compromise his concert career. When it came right down to it, since both his performing and examining work took him to many different parts of the world, the only real issue was how to dovetail the two schedules without any sort of professional compromise. Occasionally this made for some quite tight changes of plane. On one occasion he had had to sprint very quickly indeed when his plane arrived late for a connecting flight in Barbados; he had managed to make it to the plane in the nick of time, though his luggage had not but, on the whole, he was able to fulfil his responsibilities efficiently and effectively.

As Chief Examiner, part of his role was to be chairman of the interviewing panel for all prospective new examiners. For any potential applicant the process was rigorous and thorough, and many did not get through, even on a second or third attempt.

Today, the panel of five, including himself, had so far seen four applicants and, whilst all of them had looked promising on paper, none of them had impressed at interview, and there was a definite air of negativity in the room. Now it was the turn of the fifth. With a sigh, Marcus took the next folder from the top of the pile, quickly skimmed through the details one final time, looked round at his fellow panel members to make sure everyone was ready, then nodded to the secretary who opened the door.

"Joshua McDaniel", she announced, as he stepped over the threshold.

As the slim young man approached the desk Marcus stood up to shake his hand, but as the two of them made eye contact there was a slight pause, followed by a stirring of memory, and then a moment of recognition. It was Josh who made the connection first, although his exclamation did lack a certain amount of detail.

"Good gracious!" he stammered, "It's you!"

The Chief Examiner chuckled. "Yes, it's me. Now just remind me, where have we met before?"

"Quite a few years ago you were my examiner when I took my Grade eight; and afterwards, although I have to admit I may have been guilty of a slight breach of protocol, I asked you to tell me how I could become an examiner."

"Ah yes, now I do remember!"

"Well, I listened to your advice, and here I am! At least, I hope I'll be here, if you see what I mean."

"Well, let's find out shall we?"

Marcus introduced the other members of the panel to Josh, before motioning to him to take a seat, and the interview began.

♦ ♦ ♦

Just off Gerard Street, in London's Chinatown, lies a narrow alleyway which tourists seldom explore. It is little wonder that your average holiday maker does not venture into it – there is nothing attractive about it whatsoever. It is dirty and it stinks. The dubious businesses which ply their trades here, together with other related 'activities', are known to the police; but, since the various goings-on are kept very much within the immediate locality, and seem to be adequately controlled by the locals themselves, they are generally ignored by the authorities.

At the very end of this unappealing alley, next to a row of foul-smelling rubbish containers, is a narrow doorway with a handwritten sign above it saying, "Good Quality Meals". And it was here, tucked away in a curtained-off area, right at the back of this little-known quiet Chinese restaurant in Soho, that Zoltan Augustus sat, shoe-horned into a private booth, with a diminutive-looking glass of mint tea on the table in front of him. Any observer would have thought that either the booth was too small or Zoltan was too big. Someone of his vast immensity squeezed into such a tiny space behind a table that small – it just didn't *look* right. He looked like a cartoon.

But there were no observers. The manager knew better than to seat any other customers anywhere near to Mr Augustus; and, in any case, Sven stood a short distance away to firmly (but not always politely) direct people away.

Zoltan glanced at his watch for the sixth time in three minutes, although he knew it wasn't necessary. She had never been late for an appointment with him and this time would be no different. He smiled to himself, a thin, mirthless, tight-lipped smile. He liked working with professionals.

Sven took a step out of the shadows to intercept a beautifully proportioned handsome young woman who, he assumed, was making her way to the restroom. He spoke as he had been instructed:

"Sorry madam, but the restroom is out of order."

When she replied her accent was neat. Crisp. Precise. And ice cold.

"Tell Mr Augustus I'm here."

"Can I take your name please, madam?"

"It's OK, Sven, let her through," Zoltan's resonant voice commanded from behind the dividing curtain.

Sven obediently stepped aside and held the curtain open for her. The woman's dark glasses kept Sven from seeing the icy glare she gave him as she stepped through, with poise, elegance and an evident air of superiority.

She did not respond as Zoltan looked up at her and gave a curt nod.

"Hello Tatyana."

She slid into the booth, accomplishing the manoeuvre with considerably greater style and panache than he had managed, and then regarded him coolly, across the table.

Zoltan did not offer her a drink.

She would not have accepted the offer anyway.

"I told you never to use my name. I sincerely hope I don't have to remind you again."

"I doubt it's your real name anyway, so don't get shirty."

Her gaze shifted to his glass of mint tea. Though already small, it appeared miniscule against the backdrop of his overstuffed belly, an overflowing three inches of which concealed the edge of the table from view.

Her lip curled slightly as she said, "You have decided to become teetotal since we last met?"

Zoltan snorted. "Doctor's orders. Occasionally, I remember to follow them."

There was a short pause. Then:

"I suppose you know why I have asked you to come here?"

"I can guess." A gentle draught was coming from somewhere and, beneath her wide-brimmed hat, her beautiful blonde hair cascading down her shoulders flowed in sympathy with it. Anyone else would have been entranced, but Zoltan was not in the mood for niceties.

Knowing that Sven would be listening to all that was said, Zoltan raised his voice a little, delivering his words clearly. "It seems that my regular staff are not up to the task which has now presented itself." He then lowered his voice to a whisper and leaned across the table towards her. "I want you to find whoever it is that has been killing my men, and who has now threatened to kill me."

"And when I do?"

"Bring him to me, preferably alive, though that is not absolutely necessary."

"That would be more difficult...and more - "

"More expensive?" He gave a half sneer. "I understand. Don't worry, you'll get the appropriate amount."

"Very well."

"So you accept?"

She responded with a slight, almost imperceptible nod, then stood up. She made to leave, but he spoke again.

"Just one more thing. This fellow, this...*creature* has become a real nuisance to me. There have been others before, of course, but for once I find myself having to concede, with considerable reluctance, that this one does seem to know what he is doing. Can you give me any guarantee that you will indeed bring this matter to a satisfactory conclusion?"

She almost left the question unanswered, but then she turned to face him, and removed her dark glasses so he could see the full depth of her penetrating stare. She smiled, but her eyes did not.

"A stupid question, Mr Augustus," she said, crisply. "I always get the job done, as you well know."

Nothing further was said. Nothing further was needed. The deal had been made and funds would be transferred, fifty percent up front with the other half becoming payable on completion of the job.

An instant later, the only indication that Tatyana had been there at all was the curtain which swung gently back and forth after she had disappeared through it.

Zoltan took an inelegant gulp of his mint tea, grimacing as he realised, too late, that it had gone cold. Sven stepped through the curtain.

"Everything OK, sir?"

Zoltan nodded. "Bring the car. We're leaving."

Sven ran off to ready the vehicle while Zoltan slowly eased himself from behind the tiny table, with great difficulty and even greater cursing.

Chapter Nine

If his phone reached seven rings without being answered it would automatically go to voicemail.

When it began to emit its ringtone (which he had selected as Wagner's "Ride of the Valkyries") he was, as they say, in the middle of something.

On the fourth ring, and wearing only a towel, Josh came racing out of the shower, counting the rings out loud as he did so. He ran across the landing – *fifth ring* - into the bedroom and snatched up the phone with his still-wet hand. *Sixth.* He fumbled for the button.

How was it possible, he thought, not for the first time, for there to be people being paid to design these amazing phones which, on the one hand, could do everything from making the tea to flying to the moon, whilst, on the other hand, were supplied with buttons so small that they could only be operated by someone with fingertips the size of an amoeba.

Miraculously, he hit the button a nano-second before voicemail would have cut in.

"Hello?"

"Hello, could I speak to Joshua McDaniel, please?"

"Yes, speaking."

"Joshua, hello. This is Marcus Hyde calling from the Associated Board."

Josh's heart skipped a beat as he tried, with only partial success, to keep himself from conveying the slight tremor in his voice.

"Oh, Mr Hyde, how nice of you to call. How are you?"

"Very well, thanks, and you?"

"Yes, yes, I'm fine too…thank you."

"I hope I didn't call at a bad time?"

Still wet, and clad in his sagging towel, Josh regarded himself in the full length mirror, noticing the numerous drip marks appearing on the carpet beneath him.

"Not at all. It's actually a very good time. What can I do for you?"

"Good. Well, I expect you can guess what I'm calling about?"

A small laugh. "I suppose I do have half an idea."

"I'll get right to it then. The selection committee has just concluded its discussions regarding your application to become an examiner."

"Yes?"

"Whilst they were all very impressed with you, they did give voice to one significant reservation."

Joshua began to have a sinking feeling inside.

"Oh? And what was that?"

"Well, you are still very young. In fact, if we were to take you on, you'd be the youngest applicant we would have ever accepted; and it is necessary for examiners to have – how can I put it? – a degree of gravitas, the kind of authority which is generally only acquired with age."

As he continued to listen, Joshua's head dropped to his chest.

"However," Marcus continued, "in view of the outstanding impression you made at your interview, together with your wealth of musical knowledge and experience, the committee felt that, on this occasion, they would be willing to overlook your tender years. So, that being the case, we would be delighted if you would consider starting your examiner training with us at the next available opportunity."

"Hey, that's fantastic! Very good news indeed."

"Can I take that as a 'yes' then?"

"Indeed you can. Thank you very much."

"However, I have to advise you that simply embarking on the training does not in any way guarantee that you will be invited to join the examiner panel at the end of it. It is important that you understand that."

"Yes, I hear you loud and clear."

"That's great. Well, someone from the training team will be in touch with you shortly to arrange the details regarding dates and so on, and then we can get started."

"I'll look forward to it. Thanks, Mr Hyde."

"Thank you, Joshua, but please call me Marcus."

"Yes, of course, Marcus."

"Great. OK then, we'll be seeing you soon. Bye."

"Bye...and thanks."

The call disconnected. Josh remained motionless, gazing into space, oblivious to the fact that the towel was now lying in a crumpled heap around his feet and equally oblivious to the resultant goosebumps appearing on his skin.

Just a few moments later the news truly sank in, and took root. At last, after all this time, the hope which he had nurtured and cherished was finally starting to become a reality!

"Yes!" He shouted, punching the air, "Yes, yes, YES!"

Then, suddenly, he realised that he was feeling just a little chilly...

Chapter Ten

The examiner training was tough, necessarily thorough, and became steadily more demanding as it progressed; and, as Marcus had indicated, not all who embarked on the training course completed it successfully. Having made a start, there would always be a few who realised that, after all, the life of a music examiner was not for them and would withdraw of their own volition. Others, who, as the course progressed, emerged as being below par were politely but firmly thanked for their interest before being given their marching orders.

At first, all Josh was required to do was to sit alongside the Chief Examiner and 'shadow-mark' each candidate, trying desperately to ensure that his marks matched those of his mentor. However, as the days passed he was required to take on an increasing amount of the leading role; true, it was still the Chief Examiner's result which would be the official one but, at such times, and as far as the candidate was concerned, Josh *was* the examiner.

It was unrelenting work, demanding complete and constant concentration, though it was not without its lighter moments. For instance, at the end of her Grade 1 piano exam an adorable 10-year old girl, as she was about to leave the room, paused at the door just long enough to look straight at Josh and announce, "You're *very* handsome!"

Later, when he asked a candidate who was clearly from an Indian background about the mood of a particular piece, he received the rather peculiar response, "It sounds like you're dead."

"I beg your pardon?"

"Oh, I am really terribly sorry, sir. What I am meaning to say is: It sounds like you are in Heaven."

Of course, there were serious moments too. One candidate made a single mistake, assumed he'd failed and burst into tears on the spot.

Luckily, Joshua had a packet of tissues on standby in case of such an incident, and receivedé a discreet nod of approval from the chief as he did his best to console the distraught acolyte.

At one point, after enduring some of the worst scale playing he had heard in a long time, Josh was mortified when he realised he'd been asking the candidate to play the scales from a different grade! Aargh! Why the blazes hadn't the kid spoken up? He apologised to the candidate and, now feeling as though he had probably blown his chances completely, started asking for the correct scales second time around. Marcus had just smiled.

"Don't worry about that," he said. "That's something that could happen to anyone – it has even happened to me. The important thing was that you realised your mistake and were able to rectify it."

And then there was all the usual stuff: Violas weren't properly in tune, singers stared at the floor and sang flat, guitarists played so quietly as to be almost inaudible, and so it went on.

Occasionally, however, amongst all the mediocrity a real gem would emerge. A boy of only twelve raced through the finale of the Beethoven *Pathétique* as though it were the simplest thing in the world; and a tear came to Josh's eye during a particularly expressive saxophone rendition of Saint-Saens' *The Swan*.

Mid-morning, the steward, an elderly yet very sprightly lady, brought in some refreshments – but these were not just *any* refreshments. After all, with the Chief Examiner in attendance a few own-brand tea-bags from the corner shop and some sorry-looking custard creams weren't going to do it. No, this was the finest oolong tea, imported especially from China, and the biscuits were top-of-the-range cookies from Harrod's, infused with strawberries and clotted cream. After setting down the tray (which was itself silver plated and really very ornate) she reached into her pocket, produced an envelope and handed it to Marcus.

"Someone dropped this off for you, sir. Didn't give his name, although I did ask, but he said you were expecting it, so I thought I'd better bring it to you during your break."

Marcus thanked her and put the envelope away safely, deep in his inside jacket pocket. Then, just as Joshua was halfway through one of the much appreciated executive cookies, Marcus asked, "So, how do you feel it's all going?"

He paused, using a napkin to dab the crumbs from his lips. Was there a 'correct' answer to this question?

"Well," he began, "on the whole it doesn't seem to be going too badly, although I did feel a little uncertain when I had to pass judgement on that Grade Eight bassoonist, not to mention the Grade Seven euphonium. In all honesty, I don't really know much about those instruments."

Marcus smiled. "That's a good answer," he said. "In fact, if you ever did lose that feeling of uncertainty, if there ever came a day when you became so cock-sure of yourself that you thought this was an easy job to do, well that would probably be the day to pack up and go home."

Josh was enjoying his training. He could sense it was going well and that he was meeting with approval. He could tell there was a good chemistry between himself and his mentor and, as they made eye contact, his mind went back to the time, now years ago, when this man who was now the Chief Examiner had been on duty the day he had taken his Grade Eight. How things have moved on since then, he thought to himself.

♦ ♦ ♦

The days passed and all continued to progress well.

On a particular day, at about the halfway point in the training, Marcus offered to take Josh for lunch.

"It won't be anything posh, though," he warned. "Firstly, we'll only have an hour; and, in any case, do you know how little a Chief Examiner is paid these days?"

"You mean the pay is not very good?" Josh feigned an incredulous expression, "But I was only doing it for the six-figure salary and company car. I was hoping I might even get to choose the colour."

"Yeah, right." There was an exchange of smiles. "Let's go."

The pub was clean and pleasant, and not too noisy, despite the fact that it was lunchtime; and it felt civilised and welcoming. Marcus and Josh sat in well-used, comfy and over-stuffed armchairs, awaiting the arrival of their club sandwiches. Since there was still a full afternoon of examining ahead of them, Josh had attempted to be suitably abstemious and had suggested that they limit their liquid refreshment to Coca-Cola, remarking that the caffeine might help to get them through the afternoon shift. He was therefore somewhat surprised when Marcus suggested that instead they could ask for a bottle of wine.

"Don't worry," he smiled as he saw the bemused expression on the face of his young apprentice, "it's non-alcoholic."

Non-alcoholic it may have been but it was still a surprisingly satisfying treat for the taste buds. It turned out to be a delightful bottle of Eminasin Tempranillo, a rich, clear red wine with purple hues, together with aromas of summer fruits and hints of cherry, all set against a background of vanilla, with sweet tannins and a well-balanced acidity.

Before long, the sandwiches duly arrived – and what sandwiches they were! Each was a quadruple-decker feast, set within a tower of thick-cut, hearty granary bread. There were layers upon layers of roast ham, turkey and bacon, with crispy Romaine lettuce, vine-ripened tomatoes, sweet pickles and a generous helping of French garlic mayonnaise, with a side order of light and crispy fries. They both tucked in with enthusiasm, chatting casually about numerous aspects of the examiner's role and the various difficulties involved with trying to get the marking *just* right for every candidate.

After the last crumbs had been consumed Marcus reached into his pocket and said, "I don't know whether you'd be interested, but I have two complimentary tickets for my concert next week in the Barbican. I wondered if you might like to come and bring along a friend too, if you like." He handed the slim packet across the table. Josh smiled as he took it.

"That would be great!" he said. "Yes, I'd like that very much."

There was a lapse in the conversation, filled by the gentle ambient hubbub of general chatter coming from the other lunchtime diners.

As the training days had progressed, Josh had found himself with a recurrent thought in his mind. Try as he might, he couldn't shake it off so had made a mental note to mention it to Marcus, should a suitable moment present itself; and it felt as though the time had arrived. He cleared his throat and began.

"Marcus, I was wondering..."

"Yes?"

"Well, at the risk of breaching protocol..."

Marcus' eyebrow raised. What was coming?

Josh suddenly felt awkward and he hesitated.

"Come on, Josh. Now you've begun you might as well come out with it; and you don't need to worry about my programme – I won't be playing anything atonal."

Josh gave a half smile and shrugged. "It's...well, it's kind of...personal."

"Ah, I see. Well, of course, you don't have to tell me anything if you don't feel comfortable about it."

Another pause. Joshua looked out of the window, at nothing in particular. Then he fidgeted. Then he looked at the floor. Then he took a deep breath. Then he looked up at Marcus and began.

"It's simply this," he said. "When I was growing up, my parents...well... my dad..." He was struggling to find the words and was already wishing he hadn't started.

"It's OK, Josh, take your time."

Josh gave a slight shrug. "Take my time? I guess we don't really have the time right now. We've got all those starry-eyed Grade One piano candidates waiting for us as we speak."

"Josh, take your time," Marcus said again, kindly. Gently. His gaze was firm, honest, sincere.

There was a pause and, as Josh looked across at his mentor, he could see the genuine quality in the other man's eyes. He took a deep breath. He knew what he wanted to say but hadn't thought it would be so difficult to actually give voice to it.

He hesitated again, just for a moment, then summoned his nerve and plunged in.

"Well, it's just...it's just that when I was growing up I really wanted to have a closer connection with my dad, you know?" He paused again.

"Nothing wrong with that, Josh. Every boy needs a father to admire or, at the very least, some sort of father-figure to look up to. But, listen, if this conversation is too awkward for you I'm sure there will be another time."

"No, I'm fine, really. I mean...I knew that he wanted the best for me. After all, he spent a fortune on that Steinway – not to mention all the driving up and down to all those countless music lessons. Well, he didn't actually drive me himself, it was always one of his drivers, but he arranged it. Whenever I needed something, he made sure I got it; and yet...and *yet,* somehow, I don't feel...I mean, I never really felt - ". He couldn't bring himself to say it. Marcus said nothing but Josh knew that he had his full attention as he continued.

"Anyway, do you remember that time in the exam room all those years ago when I asked you how I could become an examiner? Well, that was the only time I felt that I'd ever been listened to – I mean, *really* listened to. Sure, my dad was there for me, all the time, no question, and he still is; but we didn't really relate, not then, not now - not properly, so that to this day I feel as though a piece of the puzzle is missing. Don't get me wrong, I know he loves me, and I love him, very much, but - "

There was another moment of silence. Marcus waited respectfully for Josh to gather his thoughts.

"Anyway, what I wanted to say was that throughout this training period, the way you've spoken to me and guided me – I just...Oh, this sounds like such an awful thing to say...but I've thought numerous times that I wish my dad had related to me as you have been doing." There. He'd finally come out with it. He exhaled deeply and looked at the floor again. "Well, that's it, I guess. It's strange, I've really been wanting to tell you but I wasn't expecting it to come out sounding like that. Sorry if it sounded a bit weird. I mean, I'm not trying to proposition you or anything."

That broke the ice. Marcus laughed. After a moment, Josh laughed too, a little.

"I'm very glad to hear that," Marcus said. "If that had been your intention I'm afraid you would have been disappointed. However, since you mention it, I've been enjoying the training too. You are an eminently gifted musician, and you have the makings of an excellent examiner; and, since you've opened up with some personal detail about yourself, allow me to do the same."

Joshua listened in shock and astonishment as Marcus recounted the devastating event in Bruciani's all those years before, which had left him without a father. After he finished relating the experience it felt as though time stood still.

"I don't think you ever completely get over something like that", he said, softly. "As time went on, I realised that although I had always wanted a son of my own, I also knew beyond all doubt that I didn't want him to suffer anything as traumatic as what I'd gone through. So, irrationally perhaps, I decided that I wouldn't have any children. Maybe I was over-reacting, who can say? But as time went by I became used to the idea and I've learned to live with it. And, after hearing all that you have just said, I want you to know that if I ever *did* have a son I would be very happy if he had turned out to be half as good as you."

Josh did not even try to stop the single tear that made its way down his face. It was a special moment, and neither wanted to be the one to break it.

"Tell you what," Marcus said, "Why don't you ask your dad to come along to the concert with you?"

Josh thought for a moment, then replied, "I might just do that. I guess the worst that can happen is he says no."

Marcus stood up.

"Good. Well, we'd best be heading back. Can I leave you to find your way? I just need to go and collect something and I'll see you there in a few minutes."

"Sure, that's fine."

They stepped out of the pub into a fine drizzle that had begun to fall while they were having lunch. Josh turned up his collar. "See you in a few minutes," he said. Marcus nodded, and the two men walked in opposite directions.

♦ ♦ ♦

Marcus walked quickly to the station and entered the left luggage area. Standing between rows of tall metal lockers, he reached into his pocket and removed the envelope, which had been passed to him earlier. Opening it, he removed the numbered key from inside. He located the corresponding locker and, after checking that no one else was nearby, inserted the key in the lock and opened the door. Inside was a medium-sized unmarked manila envelope. He quickly slid it into his coat pocket and briskly made his way back to the exam venue.

♦ ♦ ♦

The harpist was an adult. In music exams, adult candidates were always the most nervous. Whereas children tended to just breeze into the room and get on with it, adults would have to adjust the piano stool so that it was *just* the right height, or they would need to position the music stand in *exactly* the right place, and *then* they would have to pause to blow their nose...and so it went on. In this case, the woman's fingers were trembling so much she could barely contact the strings. She thought she was going to faint and had to leave the room half-way through to fetch a glass of water. When the exam finally finished, she looked up with a face as white as a minim and said, "Oh, I'm so glad that's over. That was harder work than having a baby!"

"Well," said Joshua, with a little smile, "I'm afraid I can't really comment on that!"

The candidate left the room. Marcus and Josh managed to maintain their professional composure until the door was safely closed, before they both collapsed into giggles.

◆ ◆ ◆

That same evening, in the seclusion of his hotel room with the door locked and with the 'Do not Disturb' sign prominently displayed, the assassin sat at the desk and looked at the medium-sized unmarked manila envelope for a long moment. He relished the moment of anticipation that always accompanied the start of a new mission and he was confident that The Professor would have been just as thorough as always in double checking all the relevant facts, details and locations and in making all the necessary preparations.

He decided that he had waited long enough, and now it was time to discover his next assignment. He took a deep breath and picked up the envelope. Slowly, almost reverently, he pulled back the adhesive flap and removed the plastic folder which was inside. He dropped the envelope on the floor and set the folder on the desk, squarely and neatly in front of him. The moment had come. He reached out and opened the folder – and, despite being a consummate professional, he audibly gasped.

As always, the folder contained numerous pages of pictures, information, phone numbers and email addresses; but sitting atop it all was a photograph. True, it was a somewhat grainy black-and-white image and not altogether clear, but there was no mistaking its identity. As the assassin continued to stare at the pock-marked face, its eyes burned deeply into his own.

It was a picture of Zoltan Augustus.

Chapter Eleven

With only a few moments to go before he was to step out onto the stage and into the spotlight, the assassin checked the fine-tuning of his EB Jones concert guitar one final time, before moving from the corridor into the darkness of the stage wings.

He loved this moment – the darkness which enveloped him seemed to be, somehow, protecting.

The stage technician, standing a short distance away by the lighting control console received a message via his headset. "We have clearance. Are you ready to go on?"

The guitarist nodded. The technician smiled, and slowly dimmed the house lights. As he did so, the chatter of the audience diminished to a reverent and expectant hush. The technician then pushed a button and the pre-recorded announcement was broadcast to the waiting crowd:

"Ladies and gentlemen, good evening and a very warm welcome to the London Barbican. For the benefit of both the performer and your fellow audience members, please take a moment to ensure that your mobile phone is switched off. Thank you. And now, here to begin tonight's performance with the world famous "Recuerdos de la Alhambra" by Francisco Tarrega, please welcome...Marcus Hyde!"

The applause, which welcomed Marcus as he strode confidently and purposefully onto the platform, was tumultuous. He walked into the spotlight, looked out into his audience and beamed. He bowed deeply, and humbly, and the crowd loved him. He settled himself on the leather upholstered antique-looking stool and, as the applause subsided, focused his concentration.

The silence became palpable.

He waited.

And waited.

The air of anticipation became more intense.

And still he waited.

He always remembered the words of his old teacher from many years before, "Don't be in a hurry. Don't start too soon. Wait for the moment. Wait for it." As a young child, Marcus hadn't understood this but, as time went on, he did come to realise what his first teacher and mentor had meant. There *was* a right time to begin playing a piece. A right moment. *The* moment.

So he waited.

Although fully illuminated by the spotlight Marcus could not see beyond the footlights into the darkened auditorium and it made him feel, in a way, insulated; almost as though he were in a private capsule, a mini-world of his own.

And it gave him satisfaction.

He waited.

The audience waited.

The sense of expectation grew.

The silence became almost tangible.

You could have heard a pin drop.

And then the moment came.

"Recuerdos de la Alhambra" is one of the most famous pieces in the guitar repertoire, its distinguishing feature being a silky smooth melodic tremolo, where the high notes are repeated with great rapidity to produce an almost ethereal effect. As Marcus began to play, the notes cascaded from the instrument with an enviable smoothness and beauty, and his audience hung on every one. The gently undulating arpeggio figures in the bassline which accompanied the tremolo melody were shaped exquisitely and, as the musical journey reached its ending and the final chord faded away, the audience roared its approval and the lights faded up. Marcus delivered his trademark smile as he rose to his feet, acknowledged the crowd and gave another of his perfectly gauged bows.

It was as he straightened up and looked out into the crowd that he happened to notice Joshua McDaniel in the centre of the stalls, smiling broadly and clapping enthusiastically. They made eye contact and connected for a moment.

But then, a moment later, as he continued to acknowledge the acclaim, Marcus' gaze shifted to the person sitting next to Joshua and he couldn't believe what he saw. Occupying the adjacent seat, and also applauding just as loudly as everyone else, was none other than Zoltan Augustus.

Marcus' smile froze – but only for a moment. His professionalism immediately came to the rescue and he eased seamlessly back into the role of consummate performer and likeable personality. As the applause began to subside and the house-lights dimmed again he re-took his seat, still smiling, and tried to ready himself for his next piece, "La Cathedral" by Barrios. But his mind was in a whirl. He forgot about 'waiting for the moment' and launched into the first movement, too hastily. There was no outward sign that anything was amiss but, inside, his brain was dealing with any number of questions. Was it really Zoltan or was it just someone who, coincidentally, bore an uncanny resemblance to him? If it was him, what was he doing here? Why was he sitting next to Joshua? Had Josh invited him...using the tickets given to him by Marcus? How did they know each other? Did they...did *he* know who Marcus really was?

With his mind in turmoil, he lost his focus.

And he knew it.

He knew he was playing purely on reflex.

Knew he was going to trip up.

Two bars later he blanked, tried to improvise something. Couldn't concentrate.

The music stopped.

Silence.

There was an audible intake of breath from the crowd.

His professionalism again came to his aid. He flashed a bright smile and said, "It's a good job you weren't listening just then." A relieved chuckle from the auditorium. "Let's try it again, shall we?"

He settled himself, and this time he waited.

Waited for the moment.

Pushed all thoughts of Zoltan from his mind.

The moment came, and this time he knew he was safe. He began again, and delivered a flawless performance.

High up in the concert hall, in one of the darkened loggia boxes, a lone figure sat, back from the edge in the shadows. Her dark glasses and wide-brimmed hat hid her identity. Observing all that was happening her lips curled into a tight half-smile. Marcus Hyde was indeed a professional – but so was she. She knew that no one else had spotted the momentary look of surprise that had crossed his face as he looked out into the crowd. No one else knew the significance of the presence of Zoltan Augustus. Zoltan himself had no idea she was even here. She had been shadowing her quarry for several days, watching.

Alert.

Patient.

Not like that idiot, Sven. Waiting for the clues that she knew would come. She saw the moment of recognition when no one else did. Her mind worked like quicksilver. The pieces of the puzzle clicked into place and she knew. She did not have any proof – not just yet – but she knew.

Unaware of her presence or her departure, Marcus continued to play and enthral his attentive audience, while she quietly stood and slipped out of the box, unseen. She descended the steps, and crossed the foyer, which was deserted apart from a couple of in-house staff who nodded to her courteously but otherwise paid her no attention as she left the building and disappeared out into the night.

◆ ◆ ◆

The concert ended with just a single encore. Normally, he would have given at least two, but the sight of Zoltan had disturbed him. Could it be pure coincidence? Had he just happened to attend this recital by chance? Or was it even him at all? Well, his thoughts on this matter would have to wait, for he could hear a loud group of people, clearly well-wishers, who had managed to find their way backstage and were heading his way. He went into the Green Room and just had time to pour himself a much needed glass of sparkling mineral water as the first of the group entered.

There followed plenty of back-slapping and congratulations - and interminable stories from a sweet blue-rinsed old lady about so-and-so's 6-year-old niece who had just started to play the guitar and who was already showing great talent after only a few lessons.

"Oh really? How interesting."

And then, just when he thought he would be suffocated by autograph hunters, Joshua materialised and somehow managed to shoulder his way through the mob. A familiar face at last.

"Marcus, that was great. Really enjoyed it!"

Marcus managed half a smile.

"Really? It was...OK, I suppose."

"Hey, I know what you mean – but you know full well that stumbles of that sort can happen to anyone; and you handled it beautifully."

"Thank you."

They shook hands. Marcus was glad of the compliment, but couldn't resist looking over Josh's shoulder to see if Zoltan was nearby. There was no sign of him so he tried to appear casual as he asked, "Did you manage to find anyone to bring along with you tonight?"

"Absolutely. I brought my Dad along."

Your Dad?

"He loves classical concerts and I promised him he wouldn't want to miss this one."

Zoltan Augustus is your father? Surely not.

"Actually," Josh continued, "he'd really like to meet you, but he hates crowds. I told him that, when you're ready, I'd bring you to see him at the stage door. Would that be OK?"

"Sure. I'd like that."

It can't be him. He probably means the person who was sitting on his other side.

"Great. I'll see you out there in a few minutes then?"

Marcus nodded – and was then immediately cornered by a middle-aged man in a strange anorak whose cat, he proceeded to tell him, always liked to listen to classical guitar music, being perhaps a throw-back to a previous life; he'd read something about this in a magazine, and did Marcus believe in re-incarnation?

In his practised, and perfected, smiling manner Marcus managed to give the acceptable combination of nods and murmurs of apparent inter-est, whilst slowly but surely retreating to his dressing room. Fortunately, just then one of the ushers arrived and began to direct people to the exits.

He heaved a sigh of relief as the door closed behind him, shutting out virtually all the babble and chatter from the corridor. Quickly, he changed into his casual clothes then packed up all his things before swinging his suit bag over one shoulder and picking up the guitar case in his other hand. Before leaving the room he first listened at the door to gauge whether the coast was clear. All seemed quiet, though he was still a little apprehensive as he stepped out of his room into the now, thankfully, empty corridor and moved towards the stage door.

As he rounded the corner his worst fears were confirmed. There was no doubt.

There they stood, Joshua and Zoltan, waiting for him. As he approached they both looked up, saw him and broke into huge smiles. Marcus man-aged to return the smile and strode towards them, feigning confidence.

Josh made the introductions.

"Marcus, please meet my dad. Dad, this is Marcus Hyde, my mentor and Chief Examiner. He has been such an inspiration to me."

Marcus and Zoltan shook hands. Marcus spoke with a confidence he did not feel as he said, "I'm delighted to meet you, Mr McDaniel."

Zoltan faltered, just for a moment.

"Oh," he replied, "that is not my surname. My surname is Augustus. McDaniel was the maiden name of my late wife."

"Oh, I'm sorry. I didn't realise."

A dismissive wave of the hand. "No matter."

Josh spoke up. "Dad used to be a high-ranking government official so as a security measure I was asked to go under a different name."

Marcus nodded as Zoltan spoke again.

"Mr Hyde, Joshua has told me so much about you. May I say how very grateful I am to you for the way in which you have been guiding him. Of course, I have always known he was very talented, but even talented people will still need help along the way to fulfilling their dreams. I am very much in your debt."

"The pleasure is all mine. I only wish all my trainees would make my job as easy as Josh does!"

Josh glowed at this commendation in the presence of his father.

"I'm very pleased to hear you say that," said Zoltan. He reached into his lapel pocket and produced a business card. "If ever there is anything I can do..."

Marcus smiled as he took the card. Glancing at it momentarily he noticed that the address was one of the most prestigious in London: The Bishops' Avenue.

"Thank you," he said, simply, as he pocketed it, safely.

Zoltan spoke again. "We had best be going now, Joshua. Sven is waiting with the car."

"OK, dad. See you tomorrow, Marcus."

"Good evening, Mr Hyde. Many thanks for a most enjoyable concert."

They stepped outside and Zoltan's Bentley pulled up right on cue, with Sven at the wheel. As they climbed into the prestigious vehicle Marcus began to walk across to where his car was parked (no chauffeur for him).

Then he paused and looked back, watching the red tail lights as Zoltan and Josh were driven away.

He waited there for quite some time, deep in thought and, even once inside his vehicle, he did not start the engine straight away as various possible courses of action continued to occupy him.

◆ ◆ ◆

That night, Marcus slept fitfully. He was restless, tossing and turning, never properly asleep nor fully awake. He was in that 'place between' that he had read about as a child – the place where reality and fantasy blur and merge. Images and pictures of all kinds swept through his mind in a kaleidoscopic vortex of colour and sound, each one unique and distinct, whilst being somehow inextricably joined to all the others.

He saw himself as a young boy, back when his parents were still together. They were watching him as he played the piano. Happy times. Then, as he finished his piece he looked round to acknowledge the applause from his parents, but only his father was there. Where had his mother gone? He began to look, feverishly. Frantically. He couldn't see her. He was starting to panic. But then his father was there with an arm round his shoulder. Everything would be alright now. He began to relax. Then – BAM! ...and Marcus was holding his father's dying body with tears streaming down his face. He was aware of another presence standing over him. He looked up...into the gloating face of Zoltan Augustus with his eyes boring deeply into him, and whose broad smile suddenly broke into a peal of raucous maniacal laughter, as he pointed across the room...and there was Josh, his protégé, playing a twisted, perverted parody of the Mephisto Waltz with an appearance and expression which could only be described as a mixture of complete concentration and utter despair. The music be-came louder and more dissonant; Zoltan's laughter grew more abrasive and insane. The colours of the room began to shift with a life of their own, moving and rolling into each other...he was crouching on a roof, peering through crosshairs. Yet more swirling and spinning. Zoltan was in his sights. His finger curled around the trigger...just as Zoltan turned and looked straight at him – only it wasn't Zoltan anymore, but Josh! The kaleidoscope twisted and turned still further...faster and faster...his knuckle whitened as he began to squeeze the trigger...Josh's face filled his vision as the weapon discharged its deadly load -

"Aaaaargh!" Marcus gave a cry and sat up sharply in his bed. His heartbeat was rapid. Beads of sweat stood out on his forehead and his breathing was short and laboured. Alone in his darkened room he forced himself to take slow deep breaths. It was quite some time before he managed to drift off to sleep again and, when he finally awoke, he felt as though he hadn't managed to obtain any rest at all.

Chapter Twelve

"Let's make a start, then. Could we have C major, hands together, legato."

The candidate nodded, gave a nervous smile and began. The scale was rather lumpy and uneven in both tempo and touch but she obviously knew how it went, and at least it was cohesive.

"Thank you. Now B flat major, staccato."

It was very rare for Marcus Hyde to lose his focus. However, as he sat observing Joshua continuing his training, and as he tried desperately to stay objective, his mind was whirling.

He still couldn't quite believe it. Zoltan Augustus was Josh's father. His father - his *father?*

"G harmonic minor, legato."

This...this *monster*...this embodiment of evil who had deprived him of his own father all those years ago was not only his next target, but was also himself the father of the young man whom he had come to regard almost as his own son.

"...and now we'll move on to the arpeggios. D major, four octaves, please."

His father?

Marcus' mind drifted back to their recent conversation in the pub. He recalled that moment of rare masculine tenderness and male bonding when the solitary tear had trickled down Joshua's face.

"Well, we've made it to the tea-break. Fancy a cuppa?"

Marcus was jolted out of his reverie and only then noticed that the exam had ended and the candidate had left the room.

"Hmm? Oh, sorry, for a moment I was miles away."

"What? You mean you didn't witness my superlative example of ex-aminorial prowess?"

Josh smiled and Marcus reciprocated, re-assuming his professional demeanour.

"What I meant was, you're now getting so good at it I know I don't have to be paying such close attention every second of the time." In fact, however, he should not have allowed his concentration to slide like that, and he knew it.

"Ah, you're too kind."

"Less of the sarcasm, please," in a mock serious tone. "Anyway, yes, please pour some tea for me, while I go to the washroom."

♦ ♦ ♦

Marcus stared at his reflection in the washroom mirror.

"Focus," he told himself, "focus."

All that training. Now it was being sorely tested. And yet, it was precisely moments like these that he had been trained to face and overcome. Nothing could be allowed to interfere with his professionalism where a mission was concerned. Nothing. Zoltan Augustus had been directly responsible for the death of his father and that account would soon be settled.

...and yet...

For the millionth time he thought back to the day when he had wept over the body of his murdered father. Then he thought of Joshua, full of hope for the future, waiting for him right now in the exam room. He leaned heavily on the washbasin and stared miserably into the plughole.

♦ ♦ ♦

"I've poured your tea," said Josh. "It's Jasmine this time - and you must try one of these fantastic choccy bics. They're the really posh kind, made with 70% cocoa. At least, that's what I read on the label – it's not like I possess a sophisticated educated palate or anything!"

Marcus managed a smile as he re-entered the exam room.

"Oh, by the way, my dad wanted me to ask you whether you might like to join us for dinner this evening."

"Erm..." Marcus hesitated, but his mind was working quickly, as he turned over the various possibilities which this unexpected invitation provided.

"I assume you still have his card, so you know the address; and, in case it helps to persuade you, I can tell you that my dad is accustomed to doing himself well – if you do decide to come it'll be a terrific meal."

"Hmmm...I'd really like to," Marcus replied, "but I'm afraid I still have some preparation to do for my next recital, and I also need to make a start on looking through some new music for a recording that's coming up."

"Oh, that's a pity, but not to worry – I'm sure there'll be other times. I couldn't have arrived until late anyway, and my dad is quite used to dining alone."

"But do thank your father for me." He paused for moment before adding, "And I do hope we will be able to meet again before too long."

"Sure, I'll pass the message on."

"Oh, and might you be free to come into the office tomorrow morning to talk through some of your exam papers? Say 10.30?"

"Certainly. I'll look forward to it."

There was a polite knock and the exam steward put his head round the door.

"Are you ready for the next candidate, gentlemen?"

"Yes, let battle re-commence!" said Josh. The two men took their places and the day of exams continued.

◆ ◆ ◆

It was dark and the sky was filled with clouds. There was no moon, and no starlight could be seen.

Just the way the assassin liked it.

Having learned that Zoltan would be dining alone, a simple phone call to the Professor followed by a short wait yielded the information he needed – the house in the adjoining grounds, apparently owned by a wealthy Arab, had been standing empty for months.

So now, clothed completely in black, with only a narrow eye slit exposed, he lay flat on one of the numerous balconies, carefully positioning his weapon between the low pillars supporting the balustrade and bringing it to bear on the dining room window of the residence opposite.

The Parker-Hale M85 rifle is an incredible piece of military hardware. Not only does it boast a threaded muzzle to suppress any flash and an integral dovetail mount which accepts a variety of sights, but it also has a silent safety catch and an enviable service record. In its military trial to become the standard sniper issue in the UK, it beat off competition from numerous rival weapons and was, eventually and after some controversy, placed second by the narrowest of margins. At a range of 600-900 metres it has a first round capability hit rate of 85 percent. Below 600 metres that capability rate increases to 100 percent.

The assassin was just 25 metres from his target.

With Mozart's "Eine Kleine Nachtmuzik" playing in the background, Zoltan refrained from feeding his flabby face for just long enough to pour another glass of the vintage Chianti Classico from the crystal decanter in front of him before resuming the slobbering mastication of his victuals. Produced in 1995, the excellent meteorological conditions in that year had facilitated a grape crop with high sugar levels, leading to the fermentation of a wine of excellent structure, which was rich in colour and aroma.

Using infra-red night vision the assassin focused the cross-hairs on the rounded yet slack features of his target. He would have to fire through the glass of the French windows but he had taken that into account and, at this range, the sheer velocity of the bullet would still ensure accuracy.

You took my father from me. From that moment your days have been numbered. I've taken your henchmen one by one to clear the way for me to get to you. This is where it ends. This is when you pay...now...

Despite his unsightly enormity, Zoltan sliced through his Chateaubriand fillet steak with an admirable delicacy, chewing the beautifully tender cut of meat thoughtfully and appreciatively, albeit noisily. It had been prepared medium rare, as was his preference, and coupled with a rich shallot and red wine reduction. A selection of julienne vegetables, expertly sliced and cooked al dente, helped ensure that the meal was well balanced. In Zoltan's opinion, hiring his own personal chef was one of the best decisions he had ever made, though it had certainly not helped his waistline - or any of his other lines, for that matter. Even now, as he continued to salivate his way through this expertly crafted main course, the chef was still hard at work downstairs in the kitchen putting the finishing touches to one of Zoltan's favourite deserts: a large chocolate and orange custard tart, on a beautifully light buttery pastry base, with a raspberry coulis and some Anzac biscuits on the side.

At that moment, nothing else in the world existed. It was just him, his rifle and his target. His breathing slowed. He was capable of a ten-second pause between breaths, to attain absolute stillness, and it would be during one of those pauses that just a slight pressure from his finger would send the blessed bullet on its brief journey at a speed of more than 1000 metres per second although, of course, an entire second would not be required.

Zoltan impaled a small roast potato on his fork, swirled it around in the exquisitely red wine gravy and regarded it for a moment before re-commencing his mastication with a quiet grunt of self-satisfaction. The finer points of Mozart, though, were completely lost on him.

Twenty-five metres away the assassin's knuckle, ever so gradually, began to bend as his finger curled around the trigger...

Momentarily distracted from his gastronomic experience, Zoltan looked up as he heard a click and the dining room door opened.

The assassin hesitated, moving the scope to see what this untimely intrusion was. It was Joshua!

He'd said he wasn't going to arrive until later!

Every ounce of his professionalism told him to abort. Leave now. There would be another chance. Yet, despite all his training, he allowed himself to think of his father, lying there with his life-blood seeping away between the cracks in the floor of the café; and, with his quarry so near, his emotion took over. He aimed again...

Joshua took his seat at the table and began to help himself to a generous slice of the beautifully cooked steak. In the background, the music had moved on to "Spring", from Vivaldi's "Four Seasons".

Once again, the assassin's breathing slowed. The crosshairs were levelled at the vast expanse of Zoltan's torso. He began to squeeze the trigger...

...and he paused. For a moment he thought of Joshua. Joshua, who so admired and looked up to him. Joshua, whom he had come to think of almost as his own son. Joshua, who right now was engaged in the simple pleasure of enjoying a meal with his father.

His father...

Well, what about MY father?

He regained his calm, and he knew that the battle over his conscience had been won. This time there would be no hesitation. The long-awaited moment of retribution had at last arrived. Once again, his breathing slowed. The aim was accurate and steady. The moment had come. Slowly and coolly, savouring the moment, he carefully squeezed the trigger.

Chapter Thirteen

At the precise moment that the bullet began its journey through the barrel of the rifle a female voice said, "Nice try."

The assassin's reflex took over. He rolled aside, springing to his feet, while in the same moment drawing the jagged combat knife from his belt.

The bullet lost its intended direction and went careening off on a completely new trajectory, smashing through the French windows before shattering Zoltan's antique wine glass and causing the deep red Chianti which it contained to splatter in all directions.

Before the assassin was fully upright, the owner of the voice which had distracted him was taking aim with a pistol of her own. With lightning speed he threw himself to one side, feeling the slipstream of the slug that whooshed past him before obliterating an ornate stone flowerpot that had been standing in the corner.

It was astonishing that someone of Zoltan's size could move so quickly. The instant his glass had shattered, a wave of fear had somehow mobilised his latent mobility and, by some miracle, he had managed to immediately leave his chair and squeeze himself under the table. Only then did he realise, with horror, that Joshua was still in his seat, frozen bolt upright, his eyes wide like a frightened rabbit.

"Josh, get down!" Zoltan bellowed.

Jolted from his trance, Josh dropped to the floor and clambered under the table to join his father, just as Sven rushed into the room with weapon in hand.

The assassin hurled himself into his attacker, who was also clad in black, his superior body weight throwing her backwards. Momentarily surprised, she lost the grip on her pistol which went clattering away across the old stone slabs of the balcony before disappearing over the edge and falling into the fauna below; but she was more sturdy than she at first appeared and rallied, lunging back at him, hissing and clawing at his face mask. Pushing her away, he swung his blade at her in a wide arc. As she leant backwards to dodge the weapon he took advantage of her shifted centre of gravity, swinging his leg and sweeping her feet from under her. With arms flailing she toppled sideways hitting her head heavily against the concrete balustrade, and her immediately limp body slumped to the floor in an undignified heap, unconscious.

Sven, seeing the broken window and his boss hiding under the table, assessed the situation instantly. Keeping close to the wall he approached the French windows in a semi-crouch, quickly yet cautiously.

With knife in hand, standing over his comatose opponent, the assassin glanced up to see Sven looking furtively from the broken window across the garden. Ducking back into the shadows, he considered. All it would take would be a couple of swift, expert strokes of the blade and his assailant would not be troubling him or anyone else again. At the very least, he wanted to expose the face of his attacker, currently hidden beneath a balaclava – he had definitely heard a female voice and that made him curious.

But he knew it was time to leave. He had already made one mistake tonight and he did not want to add to it. With practised efficiency, he swiftly dismantled and packed away his rifle before vanishing like a shadow into the night.

"It all seems quiet now. I think whoever it was has gone. Shall I call the police?" asked Sven, as he returned his weapon to its holster under his jacket.

"No. Close the curtains."

"Perhaps now you'll take my advice and have all the windows bulletproofed, rather than just the one in your study."

"Shut up, Sven," Zoltan hissed. "Now is not the time."

"Did someone just try to kill us, dad?" Joshua was noticeably shaken by the incident. The two of them cautiously got to their feet and dusted themselves down. "Why don't you want Sven to call the police?"

"This is far too serious a matter for them. They're incompetent. I will handle this myself."

♦ ♦ ♦

The Chief Examiner was in his office early the next morning. He smiled as his secretary brought in his freshly ground coffee, with a warm croissant and some of his favourite strawberry preserve, then briefed him on the various tasks which needed to be attended to, in addition to his pre-arranged appointment with Joshua.

It was only 9am. Josh wasn't due until 10.30, so Marcus turned his attention to the pile of exam appeals in his 'In' drawer. He gave a wry smile. 'Appeal' was actually just another word for 'complaint' but it somehow managed to sound more civilised.

There was a letter from an angry mother who was bemoaning the fact that the particular exam venue where her son had taken his Grade 5 did not have a warm-up piano in the waiting room.

An adult violin candidate found that the music stand couldn't be adjusted to a sufficient height. He felt sure his posture had suffered and if the result, which he had yet to receive, turned out to be a fail, felt that a full refund of the exam fee should be made.

Another letter alleged, incredibly, that during the exam the examiner had taken a call on his mobile phone while the candidate was actually playing.

Marcus sighed and rubbed his forehead.

As he was taking a much needed sip of coffee the intercom on his desk buzzed.

"I have Mr McDaniel on the line for you," chirped his secretary.

"That's fine, put him through." A short pause, then a beep. "Josh, good morning. How are you?"

"Hi Marcus. Actually, I'm not so good." He certainly was not sounding like his usually cheerful self.

"Oh, sorry to hear that. Are you ill?"

"No, nothing like that. It's just...er...well...we've got a sort of a crisis here. Something happened last night."

Marcus leaned forward in his chair.

"Something happened? What do you mean?"

"I'm sorry, I can't really talk about it at the moment. I was just calling to say that I won't be able to make our appointment today. I need to stay indoors. Sorry for the short notice. I hope you won't mind."

"Yes, of course that's fine. Thanks for letting me know. Is there anything I can do to help?"

"Not with this."

"Josh, what's happened?"

"Sorry, Marcus, I can't talk about it, not right now. I'll call you soon."

"OK. Well, I'm here if you need me."

"Thanks. Sorry about all this."

The line went dead before Marcus had a chance to say goodbye. He hung up the phone and stared into space for a long while, thinking hard, the pile of petty exam appeals temporarily forgotten.

Chapter Fourteen

A musical grade examination is marked out of a possible maximum of 150 marks, where the minimum required to pass is 100. If a candidate achieves a mark of 120 they pass with merit, but if they manage to reach 130 they pass with distinction. Some overall totals, though, are not permitted. A mark of 129, for example, is not allowed. Should the examiner find that the marks do add up to this total then an adjustment needs to be made. The examiner must think carefully and consider the overall impression of the exam performance: was it a distinction *really* - in which case he must look for somewhere to add an extra mark; or, wasn't it? Was it instead just a very good pass with merit? – in which case he must find a section of the exam from which he can deduct a mark. The explanation of the marking scheme was often one of the components of the many seminars and conferences which Marcus was frequently required to present.

It was just after lunch and Marcus was in the main seminar room, deep in the basement of the building, delivering a talk to an assembly of about sixty music teachers. The focus of this particular seminar was on not only the marking scheme itself but also the marking criteria, which all examiners are obliged to use when assessing each candidate's performance.

Everything had run smoothly until the session reached the moment that can so often spell doom for the presenter of the seminar, no matter how professional his presentation may have been: the question-and-answer section. The whole thing was positively hijacked by an exceptionally wrinkled teacher called Gladys Potts, who must have been at least 83, was far too over-dressed for an occasion such as this, and who, seemingly without pausing for breath, spent forever harping on about the necessity of authentic baroque ornamentation, whether any sort of tempo fluctuation should be allowed in music of this period, and how far examiners were allowed to let their personal preference influence the marking of such things. She went on and on and on, delivering her homily in an utterly tedious low pitched monotone. As her mumblings wore on it became increasingly apparent from all the general fidgeting in the room that the owner of the voice was the only person who was even remotely interested in listening to it. At one point, Marcus caught himself wondering whether the plight of the world might be improved if she were to be treated to a visit from his alter-ego.

The seminar, mercifully, finally ended at last. After all the obligatory smiles, handshakes and the inevitable last flurry of questions on some obscure clause in the rules and regulations, the attendees began to file out.

Marcus politely took his leave and strode briskly along the corridor, then entered the elevator and began the ascent to his office. He needed a few minutes to unwind, and his mind was filled with thoughts of the large vodka and orange he was going to have as he relaxed in his comfy leather swivel chair. He felt like he'd earned it today.

As he entered the reception area his pretty secretary looked up.

"There's someone to see you, Marcus."

"I didn't think I had any other appointments today."

"Well, no you didn't. I did tell him that you were conducting the seminar but he was adamant that he needed to see you and said he was happy to wait."

"Who is it?"

"He didn't give his name. I wasn't quite sure what to do so I showed him into the waiting room. I did warn him that you might not be able to see him so I can tell him you're too busy if you like?"

"No, it's OK. I'll see what he wants."

In the waiting room a number of high-backed chairs were arranged around a coffee table on which were a number of music journals and periodicals. The mysterious visitor had chosen to sit in the chair which had its back to the door. The only sign that the chair had an occupant was that his feet could be seen in the space beneath. Marcus entered, his professional smile etched firmly in place.

"Hello, I'm Marcus Hyde. Can I help you?"

At the sound of Marcus' voice the figure stirred, rose from the chair and turned...and Marcus found himself looking straight into the pitted face of Zoltan Augustus.

◆ ◆ ◆

Marcus' mind was racing. Had Zoltan discovered his identity? That was unlikely. - Sven was nowhere in sight and, in any case, his demeanour did not convey any feeling of aggression towards him – quite the opposite, in fact. So what was he doing here?

His smile, which had momentarily and involuntarily lapsed, returned.

"Mr Augustus! What a lovely surprise! Please come through to my office."

They left the waiting room, and Marcus gave an affirming nod to his secretary as they crossed the reception and entered his office.

"Please have a seat. Can I get you a drink?"

"Thank you. No."

"You don't mind if I do? Just been doing a seminar that has left me feeling rather parched."

A wave of one podgy hand. "Of course."

Deciding on the spur of the moment that this was probably not the time to start consuming alcohol, Marcus instead opted for the orange juice by itself - without the vodka. He filled a tall glass, added a couple of ice cubes and then seated himself across from his guest.

"I'm sorry for disturbing you at work."

"Not at all. To what do I owe the honour?"

Zoltan sat with his hands together, with his fingertips just touching his chin, almost as if he were praying, and looking for all the world like some awful distorted melting Buddha. There was a long pause. Marcus waited, patiently. Eventually, the rotund face opened and began to speak.

"Mr Hyde - "

"Please call me Marcus."

"Very well - Marcus. I hadn't thought it would ever be necessary to bother you with what I am about to tell you, but the path of life contains many unexpected twists and turns, does it not?"

Ain't that the truth?

"As the years go by," Zoltan continued, "a man in my position and with my history inevitably acquires, shall we say, a number of people along the way with whom I have not always seen eye to eye. Most of them are of no real concern to me, but occasionally the intentions of some do give me pause for thought."

Marcus maintained his outwardly calm exterior, mixed with what he hoped was a look of concern. But where was all this was leading, he wondered.

"Marcus, I won't bore you with all the details. Instead, I'll come straight to the point."

Marcus nodded.

I wish you would.

"I have reason to believe that my life is under threat."

Marcus raised an eyebrow as Zoltan continued.

"Of course, it may be nothing at all."

Nothing at all? If that blasted woman hadn't shown up you'd be history.

"Threats come and threats go. Over the years, believe me, I've experienced it all. However, even if this – this episode - is a sign that my road will soon be ending, I must say that I am not especially bothered. I've had a good life, it's true; but now, if I'm honest with myself, I'm not really in the best of health and if it's my time to go, well, I think I'm ready."

"Your life is under threat? Have you contacted the police?"

No answer, - just a shake of the gargantuan head and a dismissive wave.

"Wouldn't it be the right thing to do, in the circumstances?"

"I need to handle this my way, Mr Hyde, I mean – Marcus."

"Of course. Whatever you think best, and yet - "

"Yes?"

"Well, if there is indeed a serious threat to you, might there also be a risk to Joshua? Shouldn't you call in the police, at least for his sake?"

"Ah, now that is why I have come to see you."

He paused, as if trying to find the right words, before speaking again.

"Marcus, my son respects and looks up to you. I think you know that you have been a very positive influence on him." Another pause, and then, "Do you think that he might be able to come and stay with you, just until all this current – unpleasantness – passes by? I could never forgive myself if he were to come to any harm; and I suspect that, just at the moment, his being under the same roof with me does put him at greater risk. Naturally, I would pay you for his board and lodging."

"Thank you, but that won't be necessary. It would be my pleasure to help."

As Marcus spoke, Zoltan seemed to relax a little and the head of this evil man nodded a sign of thanks. Even the very worst of us have a human heart in there somewhere, thought Marcus.

Zoltan then added, "I should mention that I have supplied Joshua with a taser – a stun gun – purely as a precaution. Always best to be on the safe side. There are some bad people out there."

Tell me about it.

"He didn't want to accept it, of course, but I insisted. I would have preferred him to carry a more effective weapon but I know there was no possibility of him doing that."

There was none of the self-assured pomposity here. Zoltan seemed genuinely concerned. Were it not for the fact that this hulk of a monster was directly responsible for the death of Marcus' own father, he might almost have felt sorry for him.

"I understand your concern," Marcus said. "Of course, he can come to stay with me, if he'd like to. Have you spoken with him about this yet?"

"No, I wanted to find out what you thought first."

"Well, I wish it were under different circumstances, but if it helps then, yes, he would be very welcome."

Zoltan exhaled, somewhat wheezily, but clearly relieved.

"Thank you," he said, simply. "You have a father's gratitude."

I may have a father's gratitude, but I don't have a father.

"Don't mention it. When would you like him to come?"

"It will be soon."

Chapter Fifteen

"I'm going to play you a short piece and then ask you some questions about the tempo and the dynamics."

The candidate was a six year-old boy who smiled back at Joshua and nodded. Joshua began the piece, making certain that the required changes of volume and speed were sufficiently obvious. When the short piece ended, just a few moments later, before Joshua could even draw breath to ask his first question, the little boy spoke.

"Well, if *I* was the examiner I would say that you had passed!"

"Really? That's very kind of you."

Across the room, behind the desk, Marcus managed to stifle a laugh. This bright and sunny candidate was just what Josh needed. After all the trauma of the shooting incident he had, not surprisingly, found it difficult to concentrate on his work. Whilst being housed elsewhere certainly did help (Marcus had even given him permission to bring along his two pet cockatiels) the fact that he was now safely in residence at Marcus' home did not stop him worrying about his father and whether the attack might be repeated, possibly with a different outcome. Little did this cheerful, innocent child realise what a welcome tonic he was being for his examiner.

He was very small, and the door to the room was heavy. So, when the exam ended, Joshua held it open for him. He watched as the boy skipped across the corridor and back into the waiting room, grinning like a Cheshire cat. From where he stood, with the door still open Joshua heard the boy's mum say, "How did it go, love?"

No hesitation. "The examiner was really nice!"

"So you enjoyed it?"

"Yeah. Can I have a milkshake now?"

Joshua smiled and closed the door, feeling more relaxed than he had done for quite some time.

"You've got yourself a fan there," said Marcus.

"Yes, he seemed to like it."

"Often people don't realise just how significant such encounters are, especially at such a young age. That boy will remember this experience for the rest of his life. That's why it is so crucial that the experience is a positive one."

"Agreed, and if I can enable him to enjoy it even after what happened back at the house – well, perhaps there is hope for me as an examiner after all!"

Marcus smiled. "Hang in there, tiger," he said, "you're doing fine."

"Thanks."

"Have you spoken to your dad? How's he doing?"

"Yes, I've called him every day since, sometimes twice a day. He seems fine, but it must have been a huge shock to him."

A shock? Fat chance. That monster must have a thousand enemies.

"Tell you what, why not invite him to come and join us for dinner at my place one evening soon? Perhaps he'll benefit from a change of scenery."

Joshua smiled. "Hmm, that may not be a bad idea." A moment's thought, and then, "OK, I'll ask him."

♦ ♦ ♦

"I don't believe it!"

"It is him. I'm certain of it."

"How can you be so sure?" Zoltan paced angrily back and forth in his study, as fast as his unsightly enormity would allow, with the buttons on his over-stretched garments doing their best to hold everything together, while Tatyana reclined on a large Chesterfield sofa. The degree of tension which each displayed could not have been more polarised.

"The night Luther was killed, while you were attending the concert at the Royal Festival Hall, the soloist in the Purcell Room was Marcus Hyde.

Then, when your two other bozos were eliminated, guess who was performing nearby at that exact same time?"

"But...Marcus Hyde! Marcus Hyde? He's a music examiner, for God's sake!"

An eyebrow went up. "You surprise me. Of all people, I would have thought you would have been the least susceptible to any such appearances of gentility."

"But...I've met him. Chatted with him."

"When you were fired upon the other night, I surprised him on the balcony of the next house. Had I not done so, you would now be as dead as your henchmen. I didn't manage to see his face before he escaped, but his height and build were the same as those of our Mr Hyde. He is the man."

Zoltan paused for a moment, trying to assimilate this astonishing discovery.

"But what about my son? What about Joshua? I've entrusted Hyde with his well-being!"

"I don't think he will be in any danger. If anything, he might feel that he can use Joshua as bait to lure you closer to him. That could work to our advantage."

"What do you mean?"

She sighed.

"I would have thought that was obvious. Now you have the perfect reason to pay him a little visit."

"But Joshua worships him!"

Her response was measured. "He's trying to kill you."

Zoltan stopped his pacing and stared out through the window at nothing in particular as Tatyana continued, "I can make sure he is dealt with, quickly and cleanly, and without your son ever seeing anything unpleasant. Shall I get to work?"

"But why is he pursuing *me*? Before all of this I hadn't ever met him."

A smirk. "I'm sure the great Zoltan Augustus has acquired many enemies across all those years."

"I'll need to think about this, very, very carefully."

"It is in our interest to move swiftly. At this point, he doesn't know that we know, but who can say how long that will last?"

The conversation was interrupted when the telephone started ringing. It took four full rings before Zoltan was able to heave himself to within arm's reach and answer it.

"Hello?"

"Hi Dad."

After glancing over at Tatyana, Zoltan pushed a button to put Joshua on the loudspeaker.

"How is everything going, son?"

"Yes, it's all going well, thanks, and how are you?"

"I'm still warm and breathing, thank you."

Josh did not notice is father's rare and weak attempt at humour.

"Great. Well, I have a message for you from Marcus."

Tatyana noticeably stiffened.

"Go on."

"He just wondered whether you might like to join us for dinner at his house, one evening soon?"

Zoltan was looking straight at Tatyana as he replied, "Why not? I'd like that."

She nodded her approval, then said, "Make sure you take a bodyguard."

On the other end of the phone, Joshua heard what she said. "You have someone with you?"

"Yes, a business associate."

"Surely you'll be safe at Marcus' place. Do you really need to bring a bodyguard?"

"Just to be on the safe side, Josh."

◆ ◆ ◆

"Damn it, Professor, I need you!"

"No."

"Why not?"

"He doesn't suspect. You said so yourself."

"That may be true, but -"

"So there you have it. Like I said, you don't need me."

Marcus took a slow deep breath.

"Professor, I have been on the trail of this monster for years. The other night I almost got him."

"Almost isn't good enough."

"Quite right – and I would have had him had I not been distracted at the crucial moment. I don't intend to fail this time."

"So you're just going to casually bump him off in the middle of having dinner *in your own house?* That's very clever."

"Come on, Professor, we can easily sweep the scene and make sure there is no evidence."

"There's rather more to it than that. Have you forgotten the incidental detail of the lunchtime recital you are supposed to be giving in Highgate that same day?"

"Of course I haven't forgotten."

"So you're going to give your recital and then just saunter home and calmly murder someone in your own house while they're having dinner?"

"I've never had a problem mixing business with pleasure before."

"Very droll."

"And that is why I need you, Professor. While I'm out doing the concert you can be in the house getting everything ready."

"Oh, you have it all planned out, don't you - but then there's just the small matter of a certain young man who will be present. Had you thought about that?"

Marcus paused. Yes, he had thought about that, and it was the one piece of the puzzle that was troubling him. The Professor continued, "He'll be sitting there like a kid at Christmas, having dinner with the two men he idolises more than anyone else in the entire world, completely oblivious to the fact that one of them is just about to murder the other."

"There's still time. I'll figure something out."

"Yeah, right."

"Professor, if I miss this chance who knows when I'll have such a good opportunity again?"

"Let me get this clear. You are going to kill Zoltan Augustus right in front of his very own son, your protégé?"

"Of course I wouldn't be that blatant. I have no quarrel with Josh whatsoever, and I certainly don't want to damage the good relationship we have. I simply need to find a way to dispatch that evil brute without Josh realising that I had a hand in it, and I think I know how to go about it."

"You have no quarrel with Joshua, yet you want to execute his father? Hmmm. If you really cared about him as much as you say you do you'd leave well alone, forget the past and let the boy keep his dad."

"Just shut up! This is not a neat and tidy situation, I know that; but forget the past? You have no idea what's it been like having to carry this burden around for all these years."

"Actually, yes I do."

"What?"

"That's privileged information and beyond the bounds of this conversation."

There was a pause as Marcus realised for the first time just how little he knew about the Professor and where he came from. Then he said, "OK, how about this? As I've already said, I have an idea about how the job could be done cleanly and quickly, without Josh suspecting anything. But if at any time it looks as though things are not going according to plan we can simply abort and continue with the meal, and no one will be any the wiser."

"I still don't like it."

"Neither do I. Will you help me?"

The Professor's shoulders sagged slightly as he gave a resigned sigh.

"My name is not to be mentioned."

"I don't know your name."

"I know – clever eh? Protect your identity at all costs."

"P.Y.I.D, yes I know the drill."

"Well, make sure you stick to it."

"Do you have something you could wear that would pass for a butler's uniform?"

"If I say no what are you going to do – go to a fancy dress shop?"

"Thanks. I knew I could rely on you."

"I wouldn't do this for anyone else."

"You know you love it really."

"Shut up. Next you'll be asking me to prepare the meal too."

"Well, now that you mention it..."

"No. Don't even think about it."

"I recall the only time you have ever made dinner for me..."

"Full marks for your retentive memory. I won't be doing it this time."

"...if memory serves it was a rather tasty lasagne verdi. Your mother's recipe, you said. The combination of homemade tomato and béchamel sauces was excellent."

There was a slight change in the Professor's expression. To anyone else it would have been imperceptible, but it did not escape Marcus' eagle-eye.

"And, of course, if you really wanted to do the job properly, you would make certain to pair it with a cheeky little bottle of lovely Chianti Superiore."

He knew he'd won. He gave one of his disarming schoolboy grins and asked, "So...would you care to work your culinary magic once again...just for little old me?"

"I hate you, and I'm going to punch you in the face until you're dead."

"Yes, of course, and I love you too."

"Guess who's coming to dinner," he mumbled, reluctantly.

The conversation continued until well into the night, and many cups of freshly ground filter coffee were consumed. Details were discussed, and plans were made.

Chapter Sixteen

The Spanish guitar music of Federico Moreno-Torroba, much of which was commissioned and championed by the undisputed maestro of the guitar, Andres Segovia, includes some of the best known and most widely loved compositions in the entire classical guitar repertory. The "Aires de la Mancha" and "Castles of Spain" are just two of his numerous items which are frequently included in recitals all over the world.

However, as good as they are, perhaps the one piece of his that really stands out above all the others, both in terms of its musical structure and melodic craftsmanship, is the famous three-movement Sonatina in A major. Substantial and satisfying all the way through, it was a good choice for a finale. Having already completed the first movement, with its chirpy and sprightly character, and then the second, with its beautifully shaped melodies and innate feeling of poise and elegance, the pyrotechnic final movement was now well underway. Not for the first time, as the piece raced towards its breath-taking climax with its rapid finger-work and crisp articulation, the sense of absolute hush and focus from the audience reaffirmed to Marcus that this Sonatina was, indeed, a masterwork.

The concert was taking place in Lauderdale House on Highgate Hill, which was an ideal setting for a solo recital like this. Being a characterful old house it created an intimacy between performer and audience which was not always attainable in the more mainstream concert venues.

Needless to say, not only was the venue full to capacity but extra seating had needed to be brought in, in a somewhat forlorn attempt to satisfy the high demand for tickets. Even those audience members seated right at the back, on somewhat uncomfortable folding chairs, knew they were hearing something very special and would not have missed it for the world.

Further south than Lauderdale House, but not so far south so as to be referred to by those who lived there as actually *being* south, is Holland Park, where Marcus' stylish Grade II listed house was located. The three somewhat diverse strands of his career had enabled him to live well; and he had wanted to ensure sure that, when he had the opportunity for some free time at home, his dwelling was a very pleasant and relaxing place to be.

At first, he had wondered whether he was being needlessly extravagant when he had decided to buy a four-bedroomed house while living alone. However, in a sense the rooms were all now accounted for: he himself occupied the master-bedroom while he used the second bedroom as his music and rehearsal room. The third was a guest room, and the fourth –

Ah yes, the fourth...

Although Marcus was one of the most eligible bachelors around, for him to be bitten by the love bug was a rare occurrence indeed. True, over the years there had been a number of female admirers who, for a while, had pursued him – a couple of them were real cougars who did not want to take 'no' for an answer; but why – *why?* – he would always ask himself – why did he seem to have this uncanny knack for only attracting ladies of a type whose feelings and advances he was unable to reciprocate?

There had been one occasion, though, when Cupid's arrow had found its target. For one brief, shining moment a gorgeous young lady had floated into his life who was different to all the others. He remembered the very first time he had seen her – the date, the place, the time, everything. Impossible for him to forget, it was stamped on his memory forever. Her name was Sylvia and, to him, it seemed that every movement she made was like shimmering, liquid gold. From the first moment he saw her, attired like a bird of paradise, descending the wide staircase and approaching the dance floor with such poise and finesse, he had been absolutely captivated. When she smiled and when she laughed – especially when she laughed – his heart felt as though it was melting from within and he could hardly breathe. For the first time in his life since that fateful day when his father had been gunned down before his young eyes, he suddenly felt as though his life had found focus and purpose again. As the days and weeks rolled by he had even allowed himself the luxury of looking forward to starting a family with her. He had always wanted a son and now his long hoped-for future was at last starting to unfold.

But then there had been the accident.

As Marcus began the long, slow, painful climb out of the ensuing emotional abyss, he told himself over and over that in his line of work it was probably better not to become too emotionally attached to anyone. His professionalism might end up being compromised - and of course he could not possibly allow that. So, he threw himself into his work, both his music and his other more unusual activity, giving himself to it completely, determined to become the very best at each and every thing to which he set his hand.

And he had succeeded.

And yet...there was still that fourth bedroom – the one he had been saving for his son - the one which was currently being used by Josh, and his cockatiels.

Although the house itself was listed, thereby imposing strict limitations on the kind of renovations which were allowed, through careful planning and design Marcus and his team of architects had been able to incorporate a variety of modern features without breaking any of the rules. In addition to all of its exquisite décor and furnishings, the house now also boasted a swim spa, a gymnasium, an 18-seat cinema and a rooftop garden.

Outside, a man who might almost have been elderly was progressing along the pavement. It was difficult to guess his age since he was wearing a long city coat, and his trilby was pulled low over his eyes. He carried a large shopping bag and moved with a slight stoop, meaning that it was almost impossible to see his face.

All exactly as he intended, of course.

Enclosing the house was an imposing row of high wrought-iron railings, into which was set an impressive gate with an electronic keypad entry system. The gentleman paused by the gate and glanced along the avenue in both directions. Seeing no one, he tapped in the entry code and the gate swung silently open. After a final quick look both ways, to satisfy himself that he had not been observed, he stepped through onto the beautifully crafted cobbled pathway leading up to the magnificent front door of solid oak. From one of his voluminous, deep coat-pockets he produced two keys and inserted them into their respective locks. As soon as the door began to open he quickly stepped into the darkened entrance hall, immediately closing the door behind him.

Once again, the avenue was deserted.

Almost.

Parked on the opposite side about fifty yards away was a sleek black Mercedes-AMG GT with darkly tinted windows. It had already been there for several hours, its occupant watching the house closely, alert to any sign of movement or activity; but the length of time did not matter. She would wait several more hours, if necessary. There was a job to be done, and she was the epitome of patience. This quality was highly valued by all those on her list of illustrious clients – and part of the reason why she was able to charge such substantial fees for her services. She sat motionless, a slight furrow on her normally silky smooth brow, trying to make sense of this unexpected early arrival. Like this gentleman, who had tried to appear elderly, she also had her hat pulled low, covering much of her long flowing hair.

"Now, who might you be?" she whispered, under her breath.

Once inside the house, the Professor made straight for the kitchen and began his task immediately. At any other time, he would have prepared all the constituent ingredients himself, making his own pasta, ragù and béchamel sauce. On this occasion, however, there was no time to waste and things needed to progress a little more speedily; so he had obtained a packet of pasta sheets and two jars of the required sauces all ready-made. As he removed the items from the shopping bag, he paused for a moment as he regarded these ingredients, which he considered to be less than authentic, and gave a sigh. Usually he would mince the meat himself, which was always taken from the best available cut of organically reared meat, so he gave an even deeper sigh when he picked up the plastic container of minced pork (not beef as specified in the traditional recipe – pork always blended more satisfyingly with the sauce, as all good chefs knew) and tore it open. Still, there was more important business at hand than the authenticity of his lasagne verdi, so he pushed his gastronomic reservations to the back of his mind and began to set himself to work.

Marcus was nearing the end of the Torroba Sonatina. Right at this moment he was in the midst of a particularly difficult arpeggio passage – undoubtedly the most demanding part of the entire piece. There was no way he could have known that the crisp and perfectly executed rhythm was synchronising precisely with the speed at which the Professor was chopping the onions and garlic cloves in his kitchen at home. Coincidentally, it was also in unison with the gentle drumming of Tatyana's fingertips on the leather-coated steering wheel as she continued to sit outside Marcus' house, impassive, patient...waiting.

He was now into the final few bars with the end of the piece only moments away.

The onions and garlic were left on the stove to simmer and soften for a couple of minutes, while the Professor moved into the dining room to start setting the table.

Outside in the street, Tatyana was suddenly startled by a knock on the glass. A young policeman indicated she should lower the window.

She did so, and smiled at him, sweetly.

"Is there a problem, officer?"

Table mats were positioned. Cutlery carefully placed. Expensive, lead crystal wine glasses located on their coasters.

"Yes, madam, you need to display a resident's permit to park here. Do you have one?"

"Oh, yes, of course." She picked up an expensive handbag from the adjacent seat and began rummaging through it. Another smile. "I'm sorry, officer, I know I have it here somewhere."

The young policeman gave a small, polite smile and waited.

The Professor surveyed the settings and gave a grunt of satisfaction. The seating plan was critical. It was vital that each person occupied the correct seat, as they had planned and discussed at their late night meeting. Marcus would sit here, where the table mat, naturally, displayed a guitar. Joshua, with the piano table mat - there, and Zoltan, with the violin – there. Having satisfied himself that everything was in order, he then carefully removed a small glass phial from his pocket, withdrew the stopper and allowed five drops of a clear, odourless liquid to fall into Zoltan's glass.

"Ah, here it is."

Tatyana smiled again as she removed her hand from her bag and the young officer was shocked to find himself staring straight into the muzzle of a tranquiliser gun.

Marcus powered out his final chord with percussive fortissimo, at exactly the same second as the Professor dropped the minced pork into the simmering onions, and at the same precise moment when the gun gave a quiet pneumatic grunt, sending a tranquilising pellet into the young policeman's chest.

The applause erupted.

The meat sizzled.

Tatyana swiftly emerged from the car, catching the groaning, sagging officer in her arms before he could fall completely, and bundling him onto the back seat with practised ease. In seconds she was back in the driving seat, with all doors closed. She looked up and down the avenue and in all directions, at every house. No movement. No sign of any alarm or of there having been any observation. The young man lay on the back seat, moving slightly and moaning. Tatyana quickly inserted a second pellet into the gun before taking careful aim and firing it into his neck. He became quiet and still. Having taken two hits he would be out for hours and posed no further problem to her. Satisfied, Tatyana turned her attention back to the house.

In Highgate, Marcus was climbing into his car to begin his journey home.

In the kitchen, the lasagne was now going into the oven.

In central London, Joshua was making his way back from an exam session.

And Sven was standing by the open door of his master's Bentley, awaiting the emergence of Zoltan Augustus from his opulent dwelling to chauffeur him to his dinner engagement.

Chapter Seventeen

Immaculately turned out in a well-tailored butler's outfit, the Professor opened the heavy front door and bade a polite good evening to the two men standing there. As he stood aside, Zoltan entered first, carrying a small package wrapped in brown paper. The soft lighting of the entrance hall caused his many folds of flab to apparently shimmer and undulate in oscillating, wave-like formations as he moved. He was followed by the more suspicious Sven, who glanced around constantly in all directions. Sven's tailor, it had to be said, had not done a particularly good job. The pistol in his inside pocket produced an unsightly bulge in his jacket, making its location quite obvious to the trained eye. The Professor's gun, on the other hand, was virtually undetectable beneath his well-crafted attire.

"This way, gentlemen, please," said the butler as he led them across the spacious, tastefully decorated foyer and through a set of double doors into the pristine and immaculate dining room.

The large oval dining table, matching the rococo style of the surrounding chairs, was laid with a beautiful, white linen embroidered cloth. The lights in the room were slightly dimmed to allow the tall candles, set in ornate candlesticks, to achieve their full flame-flickering effect. The silver cutlery, inlaid with treble clef motifs, sparkled; and the lead crystal wine glasses glinted attractively, with the tiniest amount of the clear, odourless liquid in Zoltan's glass being invisible. At the far end of the room, well lit and gleaming in the recess of a large curved bay window stood a magnificent Steinway concert grand piano with its lid proudly and fully raised and, from concealed speakers, the opening movement of Rodrigo's famous and beautiful Concierto de Aranjuez created a pleasant, sprightly ambience.

Neither visitor displayed even the smallest indication of being impressed.

"Dad!" Joshua entered the room briskly and greeted his father with a warm embrace, to which Zoltan responded somewhat mechanically.

"I'm happy to see you, son," he said, stiffly. "How is everything going? Are you settling well into your new home?"

"Yes, all fine here. I'm being looked after splendidly."

"Good. That's good, son. I'm glad to hear that."

"Mr Augustus, how very good of you to come." Marcus had appeared in the doorway, sporting his blue velvet smoking jacket, and was advancing across the room with his hand outstretched. Zoltan made an attempt to respond with equal enthusiasm and almost succeeded. Then he handed Marcus the package which, being quite small already, appeared absolutely miniscule in the grip of one of his gargantuan hands.

"Just a small gift. A mere nothing, but I hope you like it."

"You really didn't need to bring anything, but thank you all the same. Shall I open it now?"

"As you wish."

Marcus unfolded the brown paper wrapping and found that he was holding a book with a purple cover, entitled "The Cryptic Lines".

"It's a short gothic-style mystery novel by some fellow called Richard Storry. I haven't read it myself but I gather it has had some good reviews."

"Many thanks. I'll look forward to reading it."

"Good, I do hope you get the chance."

Marcus placed the book on the sideboard and endeavoured to recover from this unexpected display of civility, as Zoltan turned to his henchman.

"Sven, you can wait outside. I'm sure Mr Hyde - "

"Please, call me Marcus."

"Of course. I'm sure Marcus will be able to find a seat for you in the entrance hall and might even supply you with a bite to eat, if you promise to behave yourself." He gave a wheezy exhalation which might have been a laugh.

"Yes, of course," said Marcus. "Please follow me." The burly man hesitated for a moment but then nodded and lumbered from the room in Marcus' wake, back into the foyer.

Left alone in the dining room for a moment, Zoltan and Joshua looked at each other, the younger man clearly admiring the elder, but Zoltan with a look of concern on his face. He appeared as though he wanted to say something, but was struggling to articulate it. Then, just as he was about to speak, Marcus re-entered the room.

"OK, your man is being well looked after. So, what can I get for you?" He indicated an impressive array of bottles and decanters on the antique Welsh dresser. "Would you care for an aperitif before we sit down?"

Zoltan surveyed the multi-coloured selection, together with two appetising platters of hors d'oeuvres consisting of a variety of spicy meats, fine continental cheeses and creamed fish, atop a wide assortment of different types of crackers and breads.

"Why not? But I don't want to imbibe too early. I notice over there on the dinner table you have a most agreeable bottle of Rioja Crianza. I must save myself for that."

"Ah, you are most observant. It is indeed a fine wine, already opened and breathing nicely, and I hope you will find it to be a good pairing for tonight's main course."

Zoltan gave a nod and a low grunt.

"So, what is your pleasure?"

Zoltan eyed a bottle of Montrachet Burgundy.

"A splash of that would do nicely."

"Excellent choice, if I may say so. And for you, Josh?"

"Just orange juice for now, thanks."

Once they were all with drink in hand Zoltan spoke.

"I wish to propose a toast. I am most indebted to you, Marcus, for taking care of my son at the present time. In this day and age it has never been more important to have friends who can be, - " He paused and eyed Marcus narrowly before continuing, "- who can be trusted and relied upon."

Marcus gave a polite incline of the head while Joshua beamed.

"My son has told me so much about you. I really don't know what I would have done were it not for your most generous offer of hospitality."

"Don't mention it. I was just happy to be able to help. Actually, Josh is one of the best trainees I have ever had. He shows a most satisfying natural aptitude for the work."

Marcus was speaking with confidence but something was troubling him. His instinct was warning him that something was not right. The affable manner displayed by Zoltan a few moments earlier had now evaporated and was replaced by an icy edge to his demeanour. Despite all his careful professionalism and preparation, did Zoltan suspect something? Had he somehow found out about him after all?

"And so," continued Zoltan, "my toast is to you, Marcus, and also to trust. Where would we be without that?" He paused for a moment, before giving a mirthless, tight-lipped smile, then raised his glass. Marcus and Joshua followed suit. As Marcus took his drink he was acutely aware that Zoltan was staring at him, intently.

As the first movement of the Aranjuez concerto came to an end, and the soulful and expressive adagio second movement began, Marcus cleared his throat and decided to change the subject.

"So, Josh, tell your dad about how all your examiner training has been going."

Joshua turned to his father.

"I'm really enjoying it, dad. Not only is the work itself very satisfying, but after all the years of being given musical training and input from so many other people, at last I feel as though I'm now able to start putting something back; and I feel as if I'm making a really lasting contribution."

Zoltan nodded appreciatively and asked, "So tell me, how does this exam system work? What does it involve?"

"Ah, I think I can help you with that," volunteered Marcus. "I'll show you a syllabus. I have a few over there in the piano stool."

As he made his way across to the magnificent Steinway he said, "By the way, do help yourselves to some hors d'oeuvres – they're really very good."

As Joshua and his father turned towards the platters of sumptuous finger food, Marcus reached the piano stool and lifted the lid. Keeping his back to them, he was careful to shield its contents from view. He reached inside and, in one fluid motion, scooped up the squat .22 calibre pocket pistol and placed it in his inside jacket pocket. Then, just as swiftly, he grabbed a copy of the piano syllabus and looked back, just in time to see Zoltan and Josh as they turned from the silver platter having chosen a selection of canapés, and who were now regarding him once again.

With a smile, Marcus re-joined them and handed the syllabus to Zoltan.

"This explains all the component parts of the exam and how the marks are awarded," he said. "You can keep it if you like. Who knows? You might even like to take an exam yourself before long!"

"Thank you," Zoltan replied, "but I think that I am probably just a little too long in the tooth to start learning a musical instrument now."

"Never too late to start, dad," grinned Joshua.

Just at that moment the butler re-appeared and announced, "Gentlemen, dinner is served."

"Great, said Joshua, I'm famished!" and they began to move towards the table.

"Mr Augustus, would you like to take a seat there?" Marcus indicated the place where its table mat displayed a violin.

"Ah, if it's all the same to you I'd prefer to have one of the other seats. You will probably think it strange, Marcus, but I never like to sit with my back to the door. Would you indulge an old man's foolish ways?"

You had your back to the door when you came to surprise me at my office the other day. Why the change of tack now?

"Yes, of course, that's no problem at all. Please take my place, here."

Joshua intervened. "No, Marcus, the place with the guitar table mat is always yours. Dad, I'll sit there. You have my place."

"Oh...very well."

A few moments later, they were all seated, Marcus trying his best to appear relaxed and keep a look of concern from his face.

"Shall I be mother?" Joshua asked, still smiling, as he stood and reached for the wine bottle.

Once all three glasses were filled with the rich, ruby-coloured liquid, Joshua resumed his seat and Zoltan said, "And now I should like to propose a second toast." He raised his glass and Joshua did likewise.

"I thought you were only having orange juice this evening, Josh," Marcus said, a little too quickly. "Shall I bring you another glass?"

"No, I had orange juice earlier because I wanted to save myself for the Rioja now."

Glasses were raised. In desperation, Marcus was just about to intervene but at that very moment the door opened and the butler entered from the adjoining kitchen, proudly pushing a silver serving trolley which glided along silently on well-oiled castors, and on which sat a truly mouth-watering meal.

"Ah, perhaps we should delay the second toast until we are all served?" suggested Marcus. He heaved a sigh of relief as they all replaced their glasses on the table.

The butler, doubling as the chef, had done a splendid job. The top shelf of the trolley bore a steaming lasagne, alongside some freshly baked garlic bread. The shelf below was occupied by a large bowl of mixed leaf salad, together with a small pottery jug of homemade spicy honey-mustard dressing. He made the briefest eye contact with Marcus as he registered the changed seating arrangement.

"That looks superb, James!" said Marcus. There was a curt nod and slight smile from the butler who, with a certain air of pomposity, lifted the substantial lasagne from the trolley and placed it with pride in the centre of the table, closely followed by the other components of the meal.

"Thank you, sir. Shall I serve the food?"

Marcus nodded his assent.

The Professor's serving of the meal was as precise and polished as his preparation for any assignment. Complying with all the rules of good etiquette, Zoltan was served first, from the left, as is customary. His plate was positioned with the design in its decoration at the twelve o'clock position while the perfectly shaped slice of lasagne was then placed, with elegance, slightly off-centre. Next, the spoon and fork were manipulated deftly to add a helping of the salad, before a wicker basket of the enticingly soft garlic bread was placed within arm's reach.

Zoltan did not thank him.

The slight was noticed, but ignored.

The process was then repeated for Joshua, each action once again being identical in every respect – but with one exception. This time, as he leant forward to add the salad to Joshua's plate, the serving utensils caught his wine glass which toppled over and sent the entire contents splashing all over the lasagne, the tablecloth and Joshua himself.

"Hey, watch what you're doing!" Josh cried, leaping from his chair as Marcus and Zoltan looked on in surprise.

Clever, Professor. Very clever.

"Oh, I do apologise, sir. I really am most terribly sorry."

The butler produced a napkin and attempted to mop some of the mess from Joshua's shirt.

"That's not going to work," he snorted. "I'll go back upstairs and change."

"Yes, of course, sir. I do apologise again."

Josh walked briskly from the room, scowling, his previously lily white shirt now a splurge of maroon.

The butler, professional to the core, managed to swiftly soak up most of the spillage on the table with a wad of serviettes before picking up the plate of lasagne, which was now swimming in red wine, and removing it from the room.

Marcus and Zoltan were left alone. There was a moment's silence, then Marcus spoke.

"Sorry about that, Mr Augustus." He gave a slightly nervous chuckle. "I suppose such accidents can happen to the best of us, eh?"

Zoltan sat quietly and impassively for a long moment. When he finally spoke, his voice was little more than a hoarse whisper.

"How long have you had that butler?"

"Haven't used him before. I hired him from an agency."

"He is clearly very experienced and knows how to do his job."

"I agree. Until that little upset he was doing marvellously."

"Mr Hyde, - "

"Marcus, please."

"*Mr. Hyde.*" The words were separated. Emphasised. Sinister. Though appearing outwardly calm, Marcus tensed as Zoltan continued, "It is most surprising that a butler who is so well practised and polished, who clearly has many years of experience, should make such a rudimentary error as to spill a glass of wine over one of your guests."

"Indeed. I am embarrassed and I do apologise. I shan't be using him again."

"Mr Hyde, Mr Hyde." Zoltan gave a low chuckle. "The accident was well staged, but it did not fool me. I could see it was no accident. You had intended for me to be in Joshua's place and to drink from that glass. Correct? What was in it? And I strongly advise you not to reach for your gun – I promise you, you will never reach it."

A small weapon had appeared in Zoltan's hand and it was aimed steadily at Marcus, who immediately recognised it as the ultra compact Ruger LCP380.

"I saw you take the gun from the piano stool earlier. Be so kind as to remove it from your pocket – very, very slowly – and drop it on the floor."

"Are you going to shoot me? Why the delay? Why not just do it?"

"All in good time, Mr Hyde, all in good time. I have a question for you. Something that has been troubling me. But before that, your gun, please. And no sudden movements."

Moving very slowly, Marcus reached into his inside pocket and withdrew the weapon, holding it lightly between thumb and fingers.

"Good. Now, throw it into the corner."

Marcus did as he was told and the gun fell into the deep pile of the carpet with a dull thud.

"OK, so what now? Your son will be back in a moment. Do you want him to see his father murdering someone in cold blood?

"I told you I had a question, and I want an answer."

"And the question is..?"

There was a long pause before Zoltan spoke again. When the words finally emerged they were identifiable as such, but were actually more of a hiss, as flecks of spittle were ejected in a variety of trajectories from his sagging jowls.

"My question is: why? Why have you been hounding me? Why do you want to kill *me?* It is true, I have made a great many enemies over the years but, until now, to the best of my knowledge I have had no quarrel with you. So why have you been conducting a systematic attack on me and my men, while simultaneously, and somewhat paradoxically, taking my son under your wing? It does not make sense to me, Mr Hyde. What has been your intention in all of this? Why have you done it? *Why?*"

There was a pause before Marcus answered, softly.

"It was one of your men who killed my father."

For a moment, a brief look of alarm passed across Zoltan's face, but then he snorted. "If that's the case, what has it to do with me? Go and sort it out with him."

"Oh I did. His name was Luther. He shot my dad right in front of me on my birthday when he stepped in to stop a protection racket – *your* protection racket – run by and for *you.*

"Are you really holding me to blame for the death of your father? Firstly, I was not even there. Secondly, I cannot be responsible for every action of my men if they feel threatened. Your father should not have meddled in something that was not his affair. Anything that happened to him he brought on himself, as you well know. Perhaps if he had he been less impetuous - "

Without any warning, Marcus suddenly hurled himself from his chair and rolled across the floor towards his gun. Zoltan, his obesity preventing him from responding quickly, just as Marcus had anticipated, snarled and fired a wild shot, missing by a wide margin and tearing, instead, through the expensive Bose sound system. The cadenza of the Rodrigo slow movement had just finished and the bullet somehow managed to jam the system, causing the iconic three-note motif, which was now at its orchestral zenith, to repeat over and over again at full volume. On hearing the shot, the butler came bursting through the door from the adjoining kitchen, his pistol levelled and ready. He only needed to squeeze the trigger once. The slug flew straight through Zoltan's forehead. His face contorted into a mask of astonishment as this whale-like colossus was hurled back across the table, arms and legs splayed in a most undignified manner, smashing his wine glass and flattening the remains of his lasagne beneath him, before slowly rolling off the edge, bringing with him a miscellany of knives, forks, plates and glasses and, finally, the recently-white tablecloth, which draped itself across him like some grotesque shroud.

It was barely half a second after the butler's gun was fired that Sven crashed through the other door from the foyer with a roar. Seeing his master flailing in mid-air and the butler with gun still aimed, he reacted instinctively and opened fire. Professionally. Precisely. Systematically. Every shot was on target. The butler was blasted back against the wall, his face twisting in pain, his body jerking under the impact of each bullet as he slowly slid down to the floor. In the melee, Marcus had managed to roll within arm's reach of his gun and he grabbed it; but with his mind working like lightning, he quickly slipped it back into his pocket, unused, and unseen by anyone, as Joshua came racing back into the room, his face aghast at the carnage which awaited him.

"NO!" he screamed, and threw himself down next to the motionless body of his father, checking for any signs of life; but there were none.

Marcus quickly picked himself up ran across to where the Professor lay in his blood-stained butler's outfit. He was still alive, but only just, moving slightly and groaning. He immediately pulled out his phone and called for an ambulance. Sven, with a final glance at the scene, turned and ran. Within moments he had reached the car, revved the powerful engine and had sped away.

Just a short distance along the avenue, the sound of the shooting had also reached Tatyana. At first she considered entering the house but when, a few moments later, she saw Sven leaving the scene at high speed without Zoltan Augustus she knew something had gone very wrong. She started the engine, did a swift U-turn and headed away from the house as quickly as possible. As soon as she spotted a suitably small and dark deserted alleyway she turned into it, coming to a halt by a row of rubbish containers. In less than five seconds, she had stepped out of the car, opened the rear door, bundled the unconscious young policeman out onto the uneven tarmac in a dishevelled heap, jumped back into the driving seat and sped away, screeching out of the far end of the alley and heading towards the motorway.

With the famous three notes by Rodrigo still blaring forth on endless repeat, Joshua was sobbing uncontrollably next to the mass of lifeless flesh that had been his father.

From the other side of the room, where he was trying to stem the Professor's bleeding, Marcus glanced across, desperately wanting to console him; but, at this moment he knew his priority had to be to stay where he was. Using a pile of cotton serviettes he tried to bring pressure to bear on the wounds but there were just too many of them. The Professor opened his eyes and smiled, weakly.

"Thanks for trying, Marcus, but it's no use. Time for me to go."

"Just hang on, Professor. I've called the ambulance and it's on its way."

"I don't think it'll be here in time."

The same words my father spoke.

As Marcus watched, powerless to help any further, the Professor heaved and spluttered, and flecks of blood sprayed themselves in all directions. He spoke again, slowly, and with a great effort. His voice was little more than a whisper.

"Remember," he wheezed, "P.Y.I.D...at all costs. Even now, right at the end, I can still be of some assistance to you. When the police come, tell them I was the assassin. P.Y.I.D."

His body suddenly went into spasm and for a moment he was rigid. Then he went limp; there was a final exhalation and his head dropped to one side.

"Professor?" said Marcus, shaking his old friend, gently. "Professor?" There was no reply.

As Marcus sat alongside his friend and mentor, and Joshua embraced his lifeless father, both united in grief, somehow the sound system had managed to correct itself and now the poignant ending of the Rodrigo slow movement, with its gently diminishing dynamic and its gradually ascending guitar harmonics, added a sensitive finality to all that had happened that evening. They both remained where they were, keeping vigil, motionless and silent until, eventually, they heard the sound of the ambulance arriving.

Chapter Eighteen

So, despite all the careful planning, what should have been a very simple, quiet mission – just a few drops of poison in a glass, undetectable, neat and tidy, and easy to clean up afterwards – became, for a short while, headline news. It seemed that everyone was talking about it. It was announced on all the TV news channels, it was debated on radio phone-in shows, it was screamed from the front pages of newspapers, and the list went on and on.

How, everyone was asking, how did one of London's 'untouchable' major crime bosses end up being murdered, and why had he been invited to dinner in the home of the Chief Examiner of such an august institution as the Associated Board of the Royal Schools of Music? Not only that, but a further victim had also been found at the scene who, as yet, remained unidentified.

The police had come and statements were taken. There was, in fact, very little that Joshua could tell them, since he had been up in his room when the shooting began. Once he heard the gunfire it had only taken him a few seconds to come racing down the stairs, but those few moments were all it had taken; and, by the time he arrived, it was all over.

Marcus, though, had witnessed the whole incident as it unfolded and was able to give the police a much fuller account:

He had been involved with Joshua's training as a music examiner for quite some time without realising who his infamous father was. Even Joshua himself, it appeared, was not party to his father's nefarious exploits. However, several days earlier, when an attempt was made on Zoltan's life in his own home, Marcus was happy to give safe haven to his son – how could he have done otherwise? Once Josh had settled in, Marcus thought it would be a nice to invite his dad for dinner so that father and son could enjoy each other's company in a safe environment. At this point, of course, he was still unaware of Zoltan's murky background. On the night of the murders, they had all been about to start having a meal together when the butler, whose references were in order and whom Marcus had hired from an agency in good faith, had spilt wine on Joshua. He had tried to make it look like an accident but it was all just a ruse to reduce the number of people in the room. So, once Joshua had left to get changed, without any warning the butler had suddenly produced a gun and shot Zoltan at point blank range before turning to aim at Marcus too. Marcus had made a hopeless attempt to defend himself by diving for cover in the corner of the room but, fortunately for him, his life was saved by the timely arrival of Zoltan's bodyguard who came rushing in and, seeing Zoltan lying on the floor and the butler with gun in hand, shot him several times before then making good his own escape. Marcus had heard that the police had since launched a manhunt for him – he thought his name might have been Sven – but, so far, he had eluded capture.

The plain clothes police inspector listened thoughtfully as Marcus recounted the events of the fateful evening, while a uniformed constable took notes.

"It would appear," the inspector suggested, "that by kindly offering to put a roof over the head of this young fellow you inadvertently became mixed up in some sort of gangland execution."

"Marcus," Joshua had stammered, confused and trying to hold back the tears, "I'm so very sorry – I really didn't know about the things my dad was involved in."

"Come here, Josh. It'll be alright."

Standing limp, with his arms at his sides, Josh stepped towards Marcus and rested his head on his shoulder. Finally, he could hold back no longer, and he wept. Marcus wrapped his arms around him and held him tightly.

"Do you think there may be any repercussions?" he asked the inspector, as he continued to console his soulmate.

"I think that's unlikely, sir," offered the inspector, "but can I politely suggest that you exercise a little more care in your choice of guests in future?"

"Yes, Inspector, I will," Marcus replied. "By the way, after the butler was shot – I mean, the man who I *thought* was a butler – I noticed this fall out of his pocket and thought it might be of interest to you."

He produced a small glass phial containing a tiny amount of clear liquid. The inspector removed the stopper and took a cautious sniff.

"No smell. Could be just about anything. We'll take it away to have it analysed."

Once it had been established that the principal victim in this case was a known crime lord, the police did not seem especially interested in pursuing the matter any further.

"Those guys have their own code," said the inspector, "and that sometimes includes their own judge, jury and executioner. Sometimes, it's best to just leave 'em to it."

A cursory examination of the scene had been made and, in addition to the small glass phial, a few pieces of broken glass and other evidence were removed for fingerprinting and forensic examination; but the police had limited resources and had other things to occupy their time rather than the murder of a villain who would be missed by no one.

Well, not quite no one.

Joshua was already missing his dad enormously.

Or, more precisely, he missed the man he thought his dad had been, while simultaneously missing all that he had wanted his dad to be for him. The combination of both losing him and also finding out about all manner of his shady dealings produced an extraordinary mixture of emotions within.

He had readily accepted Marcus' suggestion that the now dead butler must also have been the lone gunman who had previously fired through their dining room window. Marcus had taken to heart the final words spoken to him by the dying Professor on that fateful evening – P.Y.I.D. – and it seemed to have worked.

In the immediate aftermath of his father's death, and in the days and weeks which followed, Marcus was on hand to give Josh all the emotional support he needed, also indicating that he would be more than happy for him to continue living in his spare room for as long as he wished. He also gently suggested that, even though there was only one day remaining of his examiner training, it would perhaps be a good idea to delay the completion for a little while, just until everything settled down again.

Yet even Marcus, while driven by good intentions, was also aware of another element at work in his thinking: he had always wanted a son. Now, Josh no longer had a father; and Josh was now occupying the very room which Marcus had always hoped his son would have. Not only that, but there was clearly a good chemistry between them, both at a professional and social level. Even so, Marcus did not give voice to his inner thoughts and feelings, though he did find himself contemplating them frequently.

It wasn't long, though, before Josh started to show signs of bouncing back and asked if he could resume his training. Marcus was pleased to observe this, although it was a somewhat bittersweet observation, as it reminded him so much of his own tragic loss and the way he had tried to come to terms with it, all those years ago.

Still, Marcus made the necessary arrangements and Joshua's final day of examiner training was scheduled. As it turned out, it was to be on a Friday – a nice way to end the week, Marcus had joked. The important thing about the final day was that the trainee had to run the entire day, and in order to be accepted onto the examiner panel it had to go without a hitch, with all points of procedure and marking being closely adhered to. Then there would be an agonising wait while the Chief Examiner met with the selections committee to decide whether to accept the trainee onto the panel, or not. Joshua was quietly confident that he would clear this final hurdle, but it wouldn't do to start becoming complacent, he told himself. Stay focused, and you'll be fine.

So the big day came.

Josh was very excited and, being keen to do everything he possibly could to make a good impression, he even put on his very best suit which he had been saving for this final day. Created from a gorgeous navy blue textured fabric, and tailor- made for him in Saville Row, the suit had been a gift from his father, so it seemed appropriate to wear it on this very special day.

Marcus was waiting for him in the entrance hall with the Aston Martin just outside and, when Josh appeared, dressed immaculately, smiling and descending the stairs like a movie star, he had to fight to hold back the tears. He felt as though he were seeing himself back in his younger years: the face full of hope, the unmistakable feelings of purpose and destiny, and the steely glint of determination in the eyes.

"All the best," he said.

"Thanks, Marcus."

There was a smile and a handshake, after which they climbed into the car and headed towards the exam venue.

On this occasion the venue happened to be a large room in the music department of a comprehensive school. All the schools were on their half-term break, hence the room's availability for exams. Marcus had been to this venue before and, on the way, was excitedly telling Josh that the exam room boasted a rare 9-foot Bösendorfer concert grand piano, made from Brazilian rosewood. They arrived to find that their exam steward for the day, who turned out to be a very jovial middle-aged gentleman, had already been at the venue for quite some time and had already set out all the necessary signage – this was always an indication that the steward was an experienced one, and it gave good reason for hope that the day would run smoothly.

However, as Marcus had once said, while in one sense every examining day was the same: candidates appeared, they performed, they left. Job done; on the other hand, it was also very true that no two days were alike, because no two sets of candidates were alike. Each one was a unique person who would perform in a different way and respond differently to the pressure of the occasion. In other words, you never quite knew what was going to happen next.

Marcus' extolling of the piano was no exaggeration. Having first set up the room and then having treated himself to a quick play on what was truly a superb instrument, it was precisely 9.30am when Joshua, with the Chief Examiner observing, rang the bell on his desk to signal the steward, and this final and most important training day got underway.

...and it pleased Josh greatly that everything ran as smooth as silk - until just before the end.

It is a requirement that the exam steward must remain on the premises until all the exams have been completed. However, with only one candidate remaining to be examined, the steward poked his head round the door and asked, very politely, whether he could leave as soon as he had shown them in, as he needed to visit his sick mother in hospital and, unless he left more or less straight away, he would miss the visiting hours.

Marcus and Joshua were not best pleased at having this unexpected news sprung upon them, but the laws of common decency prevailed and, having emphasised that this was an exception, they agreed to his request. The steward was deeply appreciative and, before leaving, he handed over a bunch of keys, explaining that no one else would be using the building until Monday so could they please ensure that when their work was finished all doors and windows were securely locked, and could they then please push the keys through the letterbox.

With that, the steward disappeared to fetch the one remaining candidate, as Marcus and Josh exchanged glances and readied themselves for the final exam of the day.

A few moments later, the door opened and the candidate appeared – and the two men sighed inwardly at the sight of a somewhat hesitant and nervous adult entering the room to do her Grade 1 piano exam.

She was about 40 years old and looked frumpy, with long straggly hair, a slight stoop as she walked and wearing clothes which didn't suit her, didn't fit properly and had probably been acquired at the tail-end of a sub-standard bring-and-buy sale.

Professional to the core, and being very mindful that his final day of training was not *quite* over yet, Josh threw on his best, most welcoming smile and invited her to sit at the piano and make herself comfortable.

She mumbled something that might have been a half-hearted 'thank you' but which could equally have been a snort of derision.

Once she was finally seated, which, in itself, seemed to take an age, the exam could finally begin. However, if Josh and Marcus had entertained any thoughts of completing the day's schedule on time they were to be sadly disappointed. The woman could barely play two notes without an interminable pause between them. Whatever energy and positive vibes there may have been in the room shrank rapidly before disappearing between the cracks in the floorboards like water down a drain. The entire exam was hallmarked with numerous hesitations, repetitions, frequent mistakes in both rhythm and notes, and countless moments of unclear texture with constant over-use of the sustain pedal, all accompanied by an interminable string of muttered curses and apologies.

Or, to put it another way, it wasn't very good.

Heroically, Josh soldiered on and was hugely relieved when he was finally able to speak his closing line, "...and that's the end of the exam. Thanks for coming, and please remember to take all your things with you."

The candidate didn't move. There was an awkward pause as Josh and Marcus glanced at one another, and then she said, "Can you tell me how well I did?"

Josh was ready with responses which he'd picked up from observing how Marcus dealt with this sort of occurrence.

"Ah, well, I haven't actually added up the marks yet."

"Can you at least give me an idea?"

"Well, the results normally take about ten days to be sent out. Make sure you have everything with you before you leave."

"One moment," she said, "perhaps this will help."

In a single, fluid motion she slipped a hand into her shoulder bag and pulled out a small but deadly looking pistol. With her other hand she swiftly pulled off the straggly wig and Joshua gasped.

"You! I've seen you in my dad's house."

"Yes," replied Tatyana, taking aim in their direction and keeping them both covered. "Your father engaged my services on several occasions over the years. The final assignment he gave me was to find and, if necessary, kill the man who was trying to kill him. I told him that I always get the job done and, since he is no longer with us, it seems only fitting that I should send you to join him." She shifted her position slightly and was now aiming directly at Marcus.

"You must be mad. Marcus had nothing to do with it."

"You really believe that?"

Marcus stood up.

"No sudden moves, Mr Hyde."

"Please don't be so formal. A Beretta 92? You disappoint me, Tatyana. I would've thought you might have selected something with a little more style and sophistication."

"All that matters, Mr Hyde, is that it is extremely effective at short range, as you will be well aware."

Josh was starting to feel incredulous. "Do you know her, Marcus?"

"Our paths have crossed before." His tone was level. Measured. He spoke to Joshua but his eyes never left those of Tatyana. The colour drained from Josh's face as he spoke again.

"What are you going to do?"

"As I already mentioned, and as I promised your father, I always get the job done. Really, you should be thanking me. I thought you of all people would be pleased."

As she spoke those final words her eyes flicked across to Joshua.

That was all the distraction Marcus needed. With a swift and sudden movement he swept a large pile of exam papers from the desk and into mid-air, sending them flying into Tatyana's face like a blizzard of confetti. She gasped and raised a hand to swat them away, at the same time pulling the trigger. A sharp crack boomed around the room as the bullet was fired, but it went nowhere near its target; Marcus had already leapt to one side before going into a roll. Tatyana cursed and swung round to take aim again, but Marcus was already rising to his feet and, before she could bring the weapon to bear, he had powered into her with his full bodyweight. She grunted, falling backwards beneath his onslaught, the gun slipping from her grasp. Marcus moved to grab it but, as he did so, Tatyana swept one of her legs in a deadly arc, sending the gun skittering across the tiled floor and kicking his legs out from under him. He fell heavily, momentarily winded. In the same instant, Tatyana, hissing like a rabid cat, threw herself on top of him, clawing madly at his face with her long, sharp fingernails. She was surprisingly strong; and, as her frenzied attack continued and intensified, for the first time in his life Marcus suddenly realised he had finally met his match. He twisted and writhed beneath her and tried to parry her blows, but she had him expertly pinned down. Staring into his eyes with her face grim, and filled with determination and resolve, Tatyana grabbed his throat viciously with both hands and began to squeeze. Marcus spluttered and gasped as he struggled, grabbing her hands and wrists, desperately trying to free himself from her vice-like grip. Not thwarted, she increased the pressure and, with his oxygen supply cut off, Marcus knew that he was weakening. Tatyana realised it too, and smiled – a thin, mirthless smile.

"Josh," she called out, without looking up. "Josh, get over here. It's time for justice. You need to see your father's killer die."

Joshua couldn't move. Frozen to the spot, his eyes were wide and he was trembling.

"Damn it, Joshua!" Tatyana shrieked, with a demonic look in her eye, "Get over here, NOW!"

Marcus continued to squirm, but now with noticeably less energy, his face becoming an ever deeper shade of red.

"Hurry!"

With his face bearing an expression of utter disbelief and astonishment at what he was seeing, Joshua stood and slowly moved towards the pair of opponents, locked-together in a deadly embrace. Marcus, now in great distress, was starting to lose his clarity of vision. Joshua drew alongside Tatyana and looked down at Marcus.

He spoke softly. "Why do you think he killed my dad? You don't know what you're saying."

"I know exactly what I'm saying, and I've been watching him for quite some time. Not only that, but this was not an isolated attack. Your father was just one of his many victims."

Josh looked down at his friend and mentor. He had stopped struggling but Tatyana maintained her grip and Marcus was now on the point of losing consciousness.

"Marcus wouldn't do that – not to me." A tear slipped from the corner of one eye and began its descent down his smooth cheek.

"You'd better believe it, sunbeam."

Josh was taking audible, rapid, deep breaths.

"I was there. I saw what happened. It wasn't him."

"Guess again, and stop being so naïve."

Marcus was now hardly moving. Josh's eyes moved from him to Tatyana and back again, and panic seized him.

"No...no...you're lying!" he yelled.

"Just shut up and -"

There was a crackling sound and Tatyana went rigid, arching back and releasing her grip on Marcus' throat, who gasped and took a huge gulp of air, with great difficulty, as Josh continued to press the taser firmly against Tatyana's spine.

"My dad asked me to always carry this," Josh hissed, through gritted teeth. "I didn't want to, but he told me there were bad people out there, and I see now that he was right."

After an appreciable length of time he finally released the trigger and the electricity stopped flowing. Tatyana's rigid body immediately relaxed and she slumped forward on top of Marcus, her body still twitching spasmodically. Josh tried to drag her off him but she was heavier than she looked and it was quite a struggle. Marcus' breathing was hoarse and laboured, but he was regaining his strength and, through a combination of his pushing and Josh's pulling, this slim yet muscular woman was at last removed from him. With an effort, he stood to his feet and gazed down at the comatose form before him.

"Don't invade my personal space again," he said.

There was no reply — just a number of ongoing twitchings. Marcus looked quickly around the room then reached a decision.

"Quick," he said to Josh, "help me pick her up."

Josh took her ankles while Marcus had the trickier job of lifting her heavier end.

If simply rolling Tatyana away from her position on top of Marcus had been difficult, to actually lift her from the floor proved to be a Herculean task. However, after much shuffling and grunting they were successful.

"What do we do with her now?" Josh asked.

"Let's get her over to the piano."

"Why? I don't think she's in any fit state to give us a tune right now."

Marcus gave a wry smile.

"On the contrary, what I have in mind will be sweet music indeed."

The larger-than-normal Bösendorfer concert grand piano stood there, majestically, with its lid proudly raised, strangely unaffected by the display of violence it had just witnessed. With no small degree of difficulty, the two men heaved their burden closer and closer. Then, once they were finally alongside this magnificent instrument, Tatyana's limp body was hoisted up, before being balanced precariously, but only momentarily, on the edge and then rolled inside. She came to rest lying on her front, with her face pressed against the piano strings. The sensation of the cold steel strings against her skin revived her. She tried to get up but Marcus, in a not altogether gentlemanly manner, put a hand on her back and held her firmly in place.

"What are you doing?" she snarled.

"All of this unpleasantness could have been avoided, madam," said Marcus, in a mock-professional tone, "if you had simply practised your scales properly."

Before she could utter another word, the stick which was holding up the piano lid was given a hefty push by Marcus. It dropped into its position inside the piano while, a millisecond later, the lid itself came crashing down at high velocity and with a deafening slam. Tatyana screamed as Marcus, with a flourish, turned the small key and, with a gentle click, locked the lid shut.

Muffled shouts of protest could be heard emanating from within, which ceased briefly when Marcus rapped sharply on the lid and said, "Madam, you are currently residing inside an extremely expensive musical instrument. Can I suggest that you relax and try to enjoy it?"

The sounds of complaint and general scrabbling resumed, but it was abundantly clear that the piano's occupant was most definitely not going anywhere soon.

"OK, Josh, let's clear everything away, then you go and wait in the car while I call the police."

It took a little longer than normal to tidy up, largely because of the need to pick up the shower of exam papers which had carpeted much of the floor as the scuffle had started. However, once all had been gathered and put away, Josh left the room heading for the car, and the door swung closed behind him. Marcus was then left alone with the locked piano and its detainee who, thankfully, had now ceased her assault on his eardrums. He thought for a moment, then picked up his phone, but he did not call the police as he had said he was going to do.

Instead, he dialled another number. Somewhere, in a nondescript building, in an office with no windows, a phone rang. The call was answered immediately.

"Franklyn, bespoke tailoring," a voice said.

Marcus spoke quietly, to ensure he was not overheard by his captive. "Zero, zero, four, two, one, zero, zero."

"Yes, Mr Hyde. What can I do for you?"

"The cougar is contained at the location known to you."

"Understood. We'll take care of it. Thanks for your help."

He hung up and made his way out of the building, being careful to lock the doors as instructed.

He found Joshua waiting for him in the car. For a moment he paused, observing the innocent face through the glass. No one should have to experience what he's gone through, he thought. Indeed, what they had *both* gone through. He took a deep breath, then opened the door and climbed into the driver's seat. Joshua spoke first. "Are the police coming?"

"They're a little under-resourced today. They said they'd be here as soon as they could, but it might take a while."

"So, where is she?"

"Where we left her."

"But it's Friday."

"Yes. So?"

"Maybe no one will find her until Monday morning."

"Maybe; maybe not."

"But if she stays locked inside a piano all weekend – well, I mean...by then she'll be in a bit of a mess, won't she?"

"Is that something that bothers you?"

Josh laughed.

"In the circumstances, I guess not, although the experience might deter her from taking another of our exams in the future. We might have just lost a customer there."

Marcus smiled. Then Joshua's face became serious and his tone of voice changed.

"Hey, Marcus? About what she said in there – you know? – about you being the one who killed my dad..."

Marcus lowered his head. "Erm, yes...listen - "

Josh interrupted, "I know you had nothing to do with it. You have become more than just a friend, and I know you would never do anything like that to me. I just want you to know that. I trust you, Marcus."

There was a moment of silence, then Marcus raised his head and looked Josh in the eye.

"Thank you," he said, simply, and started the engine. Just before the car pulled away he spoke again. "By the way, thanks for your help with the stun gun back there – that was quick thinking."

"That's OK. Losing my dad was bad enough – I couldn't bear to lose you as well."

Marcus nodded but said nothing as he began to drive, with a lump in his throat.

They travelled in silence for a couple of minutes and then suddenly Josh said, "Anyway, how did I do on my final day of examiner training?"

"Oh, Josh," said Marcus, in an overly dramatic serious tone, "you know I can't reveal that information at this stage."

"Not even a hint?" asked Josh, with a mischievous grin.

"Well, let me put it like this: if you carry on doing just what you're doing, in just the way that you're doing it – who knows? – maybe you might even make Chief Examiner yourself one day."

Josh smiled.

Marcus smiled.

Josh leaned forward and switched on the radio. Classic FM was belting out a particularly full-blooded performance of Tchaikovsky's 1812 Overture. Josh turned the volume up high and, as the car continued on its journey, the two men began to sing along to the famous melody. As they did so, they were completely oblivious to the fact that the music was synchronising perfectly with some protracted, angry thumping emanating from the inside of a 9-foot Bösendorfer concert grand piano.

T H E E N D.

About the Author

Richard had long cherished the idea of writing fiction ever since, while still a child, he attended an English Literature event with the author, Leon Garfield. However, life took another path and his training was in a different field: he studied at the Royal Academy of Music for five years, between 1984 and 1989, graduating with high honours and a recital diploma – the only guitarist in eight years to be awarded such an honour – and winning the Julian Bream prize. As Richard neared the end of his studies in London, he helped to found the TETRA Guitar Quartet – an ensemble with which he remained for over thirteen years, giving concerts all over the world and releasing four CDs to great critical acclaim.

In his own right, he has appeared on television and radio numerous times and his many solo performances include playing before Princess Anne at St James' Palace. He has also played for the English National Opera orchestra, in addition to acting as coach and musical consultant on a number of plays and musicals in London's West End.

He composed the incidental music to Chekhov's *Three Sisters*, recently seen in London's West End, starring Kristin Scott Thomas and subsequently broadcast on BBC4 television, and his music for *Rumplestiltskin* received over 300 performances in its first year alone. Another of his musical productions, *Kennedy*, was three times nominated for the RUTAC Drama Awards. He has also recently completed a five-volume set of pieces for solo classical guitar.

In addition, to being in constant demand as a teacher and adjudicator of musical festivals, Richard has also branched out internationally, writing for the Chinese Orchestra of Hong Kong. To date, two commissions have been premiered there: *"The Fiery Phoenix"* and a concerto for xylophone entitled *"The Rise of the Dragon Prince"*. In 2008, Richard was elected Associate of the Royal Academy of Music (ARAM), and he travels globally as an examiner for the Associated Board of the Royal Schools of Music.

His musical adaptation of *"The Brothers Lionheart"* premiered at London's Pleasance Theatre, followed by a successful run at the Edinburgh Festival. Future projects include an adaptation of *"The Selfish Giant"*, by Oscar Wilde, besides a number of other chamber compositions. Richard's first novel, *"The Cryptic Lines"* has now been adapted for the stage; and his song *"Until You're Safely Home,"* having been premiered by the Military Wives Choir in the UK has since been performed all over the world, as well as featuring as part of the Canadian Military Tattoo in Ontario.

Richard is thrilled that his first novel was received so warmly and hopes that readers will enjoy his second offering just as much.

A native of the Lake District, he now lives in a leafy suburb of south London, but still relishes the occasional opportunity to ascend some of the more remote Cumbrian mountains!

For further information, or to contact Richard directly, please visit his website:

www.richardstorry.com

Printed in Great Britain
by Amazon

80340071R00079